Woody's Journey

A Novel by

W. L. Lyons III

Woody's Journey

This is a work of fiction. All of the characters, names, incidents, organizations, and dialogue in this novel are either the products of the author's imagination or are used fictitiously.

Cover art by Darleen Lyons

ISBN: 979-8-218-07233-9

Books by W. L. Lyons III

Wyatt's Obsession

Liza's Gift

Zerbo Health Remover

And Other Childhood Reminiscences

Phyllis' Prophecy

Gabby's Wellspring

Albert's Kids

Woody's Journey

Dedication

This is an odd novel. So, it should be dedicated to odd people. Not insane or mean odd, but those few who are driven by their wild imagination and who do not accept the sayings “It can’t be done.” Or “We’ve never done it that way before.” Thus, this book is dedicated to idea-odd people who drive the world forward.

Acknowledgments

As always, I owe untold gratitude to my wife Darleen. She's not only a proofreader and editor, but for this book, she also created the cover. Her patience is infinite and advice flawless. Special thanks to Gordon Lazarus, Tom Tucker and John McKenzie, all authors in their own right, for offering sage plot and character insights.

The Herald American

Tuesday, July 15, 1969

MOON LAUNCH IMMINENT!

Nation Awaits Breathlessly

Fourth-grader Woodrow Sterling Lawrence III hopped on one foot and then the other, excitement taking command of his body. "They're gonna blast off tomorrow, right father? Right?" His right eye twitched spasmodically like it always did when his mind took off.

Woodrow the elder lowered his paper, took a sip of his evening Jack Daniels, and glared at his son. "Can't you see that I'm reading? I don't need all this distraction. You should know better."

The scrawny kid hopped again on spindly legs and raised his arms above his head like an Olympic diver. "Three, two, one, blastoff! Biggest rocket ever!" He leapt as far into the air as he could. "They're gonna launch the rocket tomorrow morning. I gotta watch it! It'll be on TV!"

"The launch is supposed to be around nine-thirty tomorrow; you'll be in school."

"Noooo! You have to let me stay home and watch! I've been digging rockets and space ships *forever*!"

"Watch your language young man; digging refers to shovels, not rockets. You're going to school and the matter is closed." He slapped the paper, straightening a crease. "Besides, the Academy will probably have it on television." Once more the newspaper rose and hid his father's face.

"Did you know that Neil Armstrong is the commander and Collins is…"

"Enough Woodrow!"

Rubbing his eye, the nine-year-old shuffled back to his room. *Maybe father is right and they'll show the blast-off at school. Sure hope so.* Woody, as he was called by other kids, sat at his desk smothered with coloring books featuring space aliens, empty candy boxes, and modeling scraps. He picked up his latest endeavor, a plastic model of a Saturn V launch vehicle topped by an Apollo capsule, and caressed it lovingly. He'd just finished building it the day before so he wiggled the escape mechanism that he'd fastened last. Satisfied the glue had set up, Woody held the rocket close to his nose and examined it thoughtfully. *I wish mom were here so I could show her. She keeps going to California for some reason.*

Like always, his imagination captured him and the model became a real launch vehicle. Woody saw himself inside the command module intoning the countdown—"three, two, one, blastoff!" He held the rocket above his head and whirled about the room, his throaty growl imitating the thunder of the powerful engines. Woody felt the acceleration pushing him into the seat as he reached to toggle a control switch.

Wham! He tripped on a toy truck on the floor and fell with a crash. The model rocket skittered away, broken into several pieces. Woody stood, rubbed his bruised knee and stared at the wreckage. A tear gathered in one eye as he knelt to pick up the debris. *Disaster. Is this what will happen to Apollo tomorrow? Is this the future? Will the crew die?* Shaking, he lowered himself onto the bed, covered his eyes with his arm, and softly sobbed.

* * *

Rejecting Martha's offer to drive him to school, he waved goodbye to his nanny and jumped onto his Schwinn. Woody's stomach churned as he rode a few blocks to the elite Nelson Trelor Academy. *Apollo 11 will be fine. It has to go. It was just a silly model that I broke.* He wheeled up to the bike rack and clamped on a lock. Panting from vigorous pedaling, he clambered up the stairs to the school entrance. As usual, boisterous kids crowded the hallway, many complaining about the Academy's traditional summer session and early hour that public schools didn't have.

Immersed in anxiety, Woody didn't notice his longtime nemesis, Harold Kingster, called The King for short. Looking to retaliate for Woody's tattling about cheating, the hulking school bully growled as he planted himself in front of the rushing kid. "Watch it, Pee-Wee, don't get in my way." He planted his feet wide apart and flexed his biceps.

Quaking, Woody nervously spun around The King and ducked into his classroom. He walked up to the teacher, crossed his fingers for luck, and asked,

"Do we get to watch Apollo 11 blast off this morning?"

"Of course. I've already arranged with the audio-visual department to bring over a television. They're on their way right now. Big occasion, you know."

Woody huffed a big sigh of relief. But when he turned to go, the sight of his broken model flashed in his mind. With a grimace, he said over his shoulder, "Great. I hope the launch goes okay."

"Oh, I'm sure it will."

As he sat at his desk, Woody shivered. He nervously chewed on a pencil while he watched the staff set a TV on the teacher's desk and arrange its cord and antenna. His right eye went into its dance and his hands tugged at his tee shirt. He kept glancing at the wall clock; its hands seemed frozen in place at eight-thirty.

The teacher stood and said, "All right class, turn to page forty-two in your text and…"

Woody heard nothing else until nine-twenty when the P.A. system announced that the launch was about to go and that TVs should be switched on. The picture flickered on, showing the massive booster surrounded by vapors swirling like an evil fog. His breath came in jerks as his eyes devoured the sight and his mouth went dry as the announcer described the scene. "The oxygen vents are being secured and pressure is building…" Woody's bladder was bursting. "T minus two minutes." Woody's pencil broke with a snap. "Seven, six, five…"

Please God…

The screen seemed to burst with flames and the speaker thundered as Apollo 11 slowly rose from the pad. Moments later the announcer said, "Passing 12,000 feet. All is go…"

A silent chant began in Woody's mind: *Go, go, go…* He had no sense how long he held his breath until he heard, "Orbit achieved. All systems are go."

"Yesss," he screamed, jumping from his seat. The entire class stood and cheered. While tears of joy streamed down his cheeks, Woody reached out to steady himself on the desk, his knees shaking. Paul and Larry, two of his science-crazy friends, raced across the room and pounded Woody on the back shouting, "They did it, they did it!"

Woody's thin chest quivered and then finally resumed its regular breathing. A huge burden floated away, replaced by a profound sense that a momentous event just occurred. In determination, he clenched his jaw and silently vowed, *I'm going to fix my model; it will be my way to remember this forever.*

* * *

Woody's mind raced as he pedaled home that afternoon; visions of the launch dashed against him like the hot muggy wind on his face. *I'm going to be a rocket engineer when I'm bigger. I'll invent better fuel, figure out huge engines, bigger boosters.* Then he remembered hearing something about matchstick rockets. *Today is a perfect day to build my own rocket.* By the time he careened up to his house, he had conjured a wondrous design.

Martha, who'd been their live-in nanny since Woody's birth, greeted him with a glass of milk and a pat on the head. An excellent cook, she indulged in her craft to excess and resembled the proverbial bowling ball. She noticed that Woody had one of his wild looks again and figured something was up. With a shrug, she went back to her book.

He detoured briefly to the kitchen, snatched a handful of kitchen matches, a roll of foil, then ran to his room. His eye fluttering with excitement, he wrapped the head of a kitchen match with foil. His father would never permit his son to play with matches, but Woody knew he wouldn't be home for at least two hours. Confident, he carefully positioned the finished rocket on the edge of his desk making sure the match head didn't touch the wood. He took another match, struck it, and held it under the business end of the rocket. Whoosh! A cloud of smoke cleared quickly and revealed the thing hadn't even budged. "Crap," he uttered, borrowing from The King's extensive adult vocabulary.

After an exhaustive examination of possible difficulties, Woody snipped the heads off three matches and bundled them in foil around a fourth match. Gingerly, he balanced the new device on the edge of the desk and held a flame underneath. WHOOSH! The new design belched a prodigious cloud of smoke, sputtered an inch or two, and fell to the carpet, branding it with a small black smudge. The desk didn't fare as well, displaying a distinct burn through the varnish. "Double crap."

Worried his father might come home early, Woody decided to quit for the day and opened the window to clear out the reek of sulfur and smoke.

The next day, the teacher scolded him on three occasions for drawing pictures on scrap paper instead of paying attention to the lessons. The "pictures" were, of course, inspired design ideas for proper rockets. That afternoon, he nodded hurriedly to the nanny and resumed further pyrotechnic adventures in his room. By the time he heard his father come through the front door, his accomplishments amounted to two more burnt spots on the desk and the successful launch of a missile that flew across the room with ease. Woody ate dinner with a smug grin on his face and then returned to his room where he quietly built four good rockets. With a satisfied sigh, he put them into a small cardboard box to take to school in the morning. *Wait until that cute little Cathy sees this. She'll be impressed for sure. I hope The King will watch me launch my missiles. Bet he'll be jealous.* Pleased with himself, he crawled back into bed, pulled the covers over his ear, and fell asleep dreaming of roaring flames leaping into the air and pretty girls hugging him.

* * *

Woody's heart soared as he pedaled furiously toward school. He clutched the box to his chest and flew through a yellow traffic signal steering with one hand. By the time he arrived, the July heat had painted his brow with sweat. He slipped into his classroom and hid the box underneath his desk out of sight. His plan, refined as he conjured at the breakfast table, was simple. Quietly pass the word that in celebration of Apollo, he'd launch rockets at lunchtime from home plate at the baseball diamond. He figured the school's staff certainly would be occupied elsewhere far from the distant field. Proud of his cleverness, he'd make certain that Cute Cathy knew about the plot.

Afraid to leave his package in the classroom during recess, Woody stood uneasily in the quad, clutching the box under his arm. But The King saw him and demanded, "What's in the box, Pee-Wee? The rockets I heard everyone talking about? Mighty small aren't they? I'll take a look to see if they're worth my time."

He reached out to grab the carton, but Woody spun aside. "Leave me alone! This isn't anything you'd understand."

"I want to see what you got right now, dip-shit. Hand it over!" The King seized Woody's arm and yanked him nose-to-nose, his sour breath making Woody flinch. "Gimme!"

Fortune smiled when Miss Taylor from the office staff happened by. "Is there a problem here, Mr. Kingster? You want to visit Principal Evans' office again?" She glared at The King with hardened eyes. "Huh?"

Slowly, defiantly, The King released Woody's arm and sauntered off. "Later Pee-Wee."

Shaken, but resolved, Woody passed the rest of the morning rubbing his eye and waiting for his moment of glory. At last, the bell rang, announcing lunch period. Cradling the box in his arms protectively, he hustled to the ball diamond where perhaps two-dozen kids had assembled, jabbering and speculating. He quickly searched for Cute Cathy and found her near home plate. *Super. She'll have a perfect view.* The King, he saw, lurked behind the backstop with a contemptuous smirk on his face—a worrying development.

I hope he stays back there. Woody thought.

"Okay, everybody, stand back. Rockets can be dangerous, you know," Woody called out, feigning expertise. With wide sweeps of his arms, he stood on home plate and dramatically opened the carton revealing four small items. About six inches long, their gleaming foil bodies glistened in the hot sun. Paper tail fins sprouted on each, a last-minute refinement. Flourishing a foot-long wooden dowel, he propped it in a small hole in the carton, angled it up halfway, and set it on home plate. Gently, he slipped the first rocket onto the dowel and pointed it towards center field. Lastly, he produced a stubby candle and lit it with a match. With a grandiose gesture, he shouted, "Here we go!" He set the candle under the nose of the rocket. The kids squeezed in closer and held their collective breath. Moments later, a streak blasted across the pitcher's mound with a penetrating hiss.

A roar went up from the small group and Woody, trying to appear nonchalant, glanced over to Cute Cathy who, wide-eyed, stood mesmerized.

Pretending to look bored, Woody shot off the remaining three rockets, all flawless. More kids had gathered and several ran out to grab the spent missiles. Woody noticed that The King, scowling, stood some distance away, thumbs hooked in the pockets of his jeans.

As the kids wandered away, Cute Cathy came up and congratulated Woody, patting his arm. "You are soooo smart to be able to do that. It's simply woooonderful."

Woody shyly kicked the dust, saying, "Got the idea from Apollo. It's gonna land on the moon in a few days, you know." Out of words, he tried not to stare at her soft brown eyes, sun-kissed curls, and delicate hand. His awkwardness abated when Paul and Larry, his two scientific sidekicks, trotted up. "What a show, dude! Blew me away!" shouted Larry.

"I saw the last one fly way over third base!" cried Paul.

Awash in accolades, Woody puffed out his chest. "I'm thinking we ought to use my technology to build a much bigger rocket. Whaddya think?" he blustered. Cute Cathy nodded vigorously.

Unknown to Woody, The King grumbled and spat in the dirt. *Look at that Cathy hit on him. Fuckin' show-off. He'll get his.*

Swelled with pride, Woody ambled to class as the bell rang. *I knew I could do it. Wasn't easy, but I did it. I'll be an engineer when I'm bigger, not a lawyer like my father wants. He doesn't understand that rockets are the future. My future. He'll have to understand.*

* * *

Still basking in the lunchtime glory, Woody stood in his gym gear at the edge of a group of rowdy boys. Coach Shultz bellowed out instructions. "All right guys, let's choose up teams for flag football." Woody hardly heard a word. He had no use for sports, not because he was scrawny and poorly coordinated, but because it took time away from spaceships, airplanes, and science.

The coach picked out two team captains who began choosing. "I'll take Jim."

"Chuck, come on."

"Randy."

"Bob."

Woody knew he'd be the last to be called—like always.

While they formed up, The King (on the opposing team, naturally) slugged Woody on the shoulder—hard. "Gonna tear your head off you turd," he growled. "Even better, I got a BIG surprise for you. I'm gonna shove those stupid little rockets right up your ass."

Woody rubbed his aching arm, knowing the game would be a struggle just to stay away from The King. Worse yet, he feared whatever surprise the thug had up his sleeve.

* * *

"Woodrow, get in here!" bellowed Woody's father. "Right now!"

Astonished by the tone of his father's voice, Woody dropped a paper airplane he'd been working on and scurried from his room. Woodrow Jr. was in his office with a scowl that would horrify Godzilla.

"What is it, father?"

"I can't believe the loony pranks you come up with all the time, but this is beyond the pale. Listen to this." He jabbed the play button on the telephone answering machine, brushed a speck of lint from his sleeve, and crossed his arms over his chest.

"This is Principal Evans at the Nelson Trelor Academy calling. A very serious situation occurred today involving your son, Woody. One of our students, a mister Harold Kingster, advised my office that Woody set off rockets at the baseball diamond. Not only could they have set fire to the school, but there was also a significant group of students gathered close-by! Corroborated by several witnesses, these actions might have injured people and damaged school property. The Academy cannot tolerate such matters! I'm confident you will take appropriate disciplinary action with regards to your son. Please let my office know what steps you've taken."

With a stern jab, Woody's father switched off the machine. "Explain yourself."

Woody choked back tears and trembled in fear. "I…I…"

"Spit it out."

"The rockets were small, like this." He held up his index finger. "Didn't go far. All the kids were behind me. It was…was…"

"Go on."

"Everybody cheered. I wanted to show them how exciting rockets are – Apollo 11 and all that. They never talk about space in school."

"Didn't they show you the launch of Apollo on TV at school?"

Woody bit his lip and stared at the floor. "Well, hardly ever."

"So they *do* talk about missiles and things. That's no excuse. One more thing. Principal Evans called you Woody. That's not your name. Is that what they call you at school?"

"Well…" He shrugged. "Woody sounds… It's not so… It's kinda neat, you know?"

"Woodrow Sterling Lawrence is a hallowed family name; one you share with your grandfather and myself. You are not to dishonor this tradition. You are named after noble, hardworking men and I forbid you to go by Woody." He grimaced in distaste. "Tell your friends and Principal Evans your name is Woodrow. Understand?" Woody, now called Woodrow, nodded meekly.

"Now, about this madness at school. When your mother returns from California, we'll decide what actions to take. In the meantime, you are grounded—no outings of any kind. Moreover, you are not to watch television for a month."

"But I'll miss the moon landing!"

"You should of thought about that, mister."

Crushed, Woody tried to swallow his disappointment. He yearned for his mother who always stood up for him. *She'd understand.* He slunk up to his room and collapsed on the bed. He drew his arm across his eyes and thought about life. *It's the way I am. I can't stop trying out new things. Like matchstick rockets. Every day can be so exciting! Now I'll miss the moon landing. I bet mother would let me watch.*

The Herald American
Wednesday, December 6, 1972
Section C2: Technology Today

Last Apollo Mission to launch
First Scientist to Walk on the Moon

Turning away from clouds gliding past the airplane window, Woody glanced over at his father who was ensconced behind a newspaper as usual. He couldn't believe his father showed so little interest in the very last Apollo mission slated to launch later that night. Over the years, the public's fervor for moon landings had waned, but Woody's passion remained as fiery as ever. He'd been devastated when NASA had announced that the last three Apollo missions had been canceled. Tonight was the last one ever.

Perhaps his enthusiasm for rockets inspired his father to take him on an airplane headed to Florida. First class no less. But then again, his father had a business appointment in Orlando the following morning, so maybe that was behind his good fortune. Having turned twelve, Woody was excited about his first time in an airplane, but the real show would be the launch. His right eye began to twitch just thinking about it.

He'd sent away to NASA for information on Apollo 17 and he thumbed through a small bundle of pamphlets scattered in his lap. Cernan and Schmitt were going to land, but Evans had been relegated to circle the moon in the command module while his crewmates frolicked in their lunar hotrod inside an ancient impact crater. *Talk about lonely! Evans will have his thoughts to himself for over three days, wondering what he'd do if his teammates couldn't return.* Perplexed, Woody twisted in the seat. *What do they think about being the last men to walk on the moon, maybe for years? Well, at least Nixon had announced this new thing called the Space Shuttle a few months back, but it would be forever before they actually launched one. It freaks me out; I'll be an old man before I see another big launch.*

His father stirred in his seat and stuffed his paper into the seat pocket. "We'll be landing soon. I never thought you'd talk me into watching an Apollo launch in person. I'm not sure I can deal with its late-night blastoff. You said about ten o'clock tonight, right?"

"Yeah, but we should be there at least an hour earlier. I'm so excited I've got the jitters. Wait until I tell the guys at school about it!"

A frown spread across his father's face. "This wouldn't be happening, you know, if I didn't have that important meeting first thing tomorrow morning. Might take a couple of hours or so. You'll have to watch TV in the room until I get back."

The plane landed on schedule at Melbourne International airport and Woodrow drove a rental car to their motel. They had a quick snack at a nearby restaurant and afterwards tried to catch a brief nap. His father's snores reverberated in the room, which along with nervousness, made it impossible for Woody to doze off.

At last, the alarm clock blared and they hurried into their clothes. The trip to the viewing area flew by quickly and Woody was shocked to see an immense crowd. People were jammed in the stands shoulder to shoulder. *Maybe I was wrong. Maybe space travel is still groovy.*

A man sitting directly in front of him caught Woody's attention. The guy jabbed his neighbor on the arm saying, "I'm tellin' you, the Dolphins are going all the way. Bet on it."

Can't believe it! The guy is talking about football, not the blast-off! The jerk doesn't get it.

The Saturn rocket stood across the water, seemingly miles away. At least it was brightly illuminated and the vapors cradled the towering white vehicle just as it did on earlier launches he'd seen on TV. His father handed him a pair of binoculars and the Apollo grew a little bit.

Speakers blared the countdown, by now a routine well known to Woody. Lulled by familiarity and the rocket so distant it barely could be seen, he felt a surge of disappointment. Even that changed for the worse at T minus 30 seconds when the countdown abruptly halted. His breathing sputtered as he held up the binoculars for a closer look. Nothing seemed amiss. The speakers announced a temporary hold.

Woody's father looked at his Rolex. "This had better get going soon. My business appointment is at eight-thirty tomorrow morning and I need some sleep."

An hour and a half later, Woodrow stood and said, "Enough. That thing isn't going to get off the ground. We're leaving."

"Nooo," Woody begged. "This is the last big launch for years. We gotta wait until it goes or is scrubbed. Please?"

Woodrow sighed. "Well, we'll wait a few more minutes."

After another hour, the countdown resumed. "Thank God," muttered Woodrow.

Finally, the P.A. system blurted, "We have ignition!"

A huge glowing cloud of smoke billowed from the launch site, jolting Woody. The gantry released the massive vehicle, which rose ponderously into the air. A few seconds later, the booming, rumbling sound of the engines washed over him and he gasped. The behemoth reached for the heavens, thundering and popping into the night sky until Woody had to crane his neck to follow the bright speck as it raced upward and eastward.

"Finally," breathed his father. "You'd think that with billions of government dollars they could get the thing off on time."

* * *

The flight back to Boston bored Woody even though the stewardess found a comic book for him to read. Now in seventh grade, his outlook on life was evolving. Although he sometimes realized his wild imagination had taken on hints of realism, crazy ideas continued to flower daily. *I'm too old for comic books.* He stuffed the book into the seat-pocket and sat back. *Think I'll ask Doctor Edwards, my science teacher, if I can do a talk about last night's launch. That would be too cool.*

Back home that night, Woody overheard his father talking on the phone with a worried look on his face. He seemed to be begging for something, but Woody didn't know who was on the other end. After the particularly long call, his father guzzled several Jack Daniels and just before bedtime, solemnly announced that Woody's mother wouldn't be returning from another routine trip to California; they'd decided to separate for a while.

The news deeply troubled Woody so he tried to talk to his father about it, but got nowhere. As youngsters often do, he imagined wild, terrible things that might be happening between his parents. All his life he'd taken comfort from his mother to make up for his father's remoteness. The thought she wasn't on her way home terrified him. He wondered if he was to blame.

His stomach churned as he tried to shove aside his worries. In the late-night darkness, the Apollo made another appearance in his mind. Agonies about his mother slipped away as he began making plans for a speech about the launch. He decided to use his Saturn model as a prop should the teacher give him a go-ahead. He smiled when he recalled his vow to keep the model as a reminder of the glory of the first moon landing.

The weekend trudged slowly by. Woody, not even knowing if he'd get permission to do a talk for his class, jotted notes and rehearsed in front of a mirror. The more confident he got, the bolder his imagination became. *I'll dazzle 'em. They'll all want to be astronauts. Maybe I'll be a world-famous professor showing miracles of science to thousands of kids. Better yet, a super scientist and inventor of atomic powered rockets. No, no, no. I'll be the first man on Mars. Too bad Cute Cathy isn't in my science class to see me do my thing.*

That Monday, Woody bolted from bed at six in the morning, inhaled a bowl of corn flakes, and dashed to school before the sun chased the deep shadows from the streets. He'd rejected Martha's offer to drive him to school, indulging his passion for cycling. Instead, he bundled up in a heavy jacket defying the winter cold. At school, he paced back and forth in front of his science classroom door waiting for his teacher to show up. At last, Doctor Edwards appeared and Woody rabidly babbled his plans for doing a talk during class. Bobbing his head and grinning at Woody's enthusiasm, Edwards gave Woody permission. "Give me a week or so to clear my calendar, okay?" He started to walk away, but turned saying, "Too bad you have to miss the moon landing today. It's happening early this afternoon, but you'll be in class."

Woody walked away smirking, knowing he had an easy solution. The landing was scheduled to happen right in the middle of P.E., his last class of the day. Two things ran through his mind: The King always found ways to make him miserable during gym, and Martha was the only one at home. His mother and father hadn't reconciled their differences and she remained in California. As always, his father was at work. The solution was obvious—cut gym.

He sidled alongside his bike, unlocked it while looking over his shoulder for signs of The King or teachers, and then hurled himself onto the seat. In a flash, he was out of sight. Winter murk chilled him and a paltry mist painted his forehead, but oblivious, he pedaled on. Quietly, he snuck in the back door hoping to avoid the nanny, but Martha was there, emptying the dishwasher. "You're home early. What's the matter?"

"Don't feel so good. Headache," he lied.

"Get out of those damp clothes and I'll bring some aspirin."

He decided that aspirin couldn't hurt anybody and said, "That will be good." While trotting to his room, he checked his watch. *Plenty of time*. He slipped into his sweats and flipped on the TV, happy that his father allowed one in his room. Martha arrived with two tablets and a glass of water. Deviously rubbing his temple, Woody swallowed the offering. "Thanks."

"You watch too much TV. Don't you have schoolwork to do?"

She sounds just like my father. "Nah. Things really get slow just before Christmas. I'm all caught up."

With a skeptical glance, Martha left the room.

Woody cradled his Saturn V model and fastened his eyes on the screen, fascinated. He rubbed his fluttering eye as the lunar module descended, finally blowing moon dust as it settled in place. *They're all safe. Bet those mice, Fe, Fi, Fo, Fum, and Phooey would rather be on the moon instead of doing laps around the moon with Evans.* His chest swelled with pride as he devoured the post-landing chatter from the astronauts. Emotionally, he kissed his model Saturn rocket and wished his mother were there to see his joy.

A week later, school once again interfered with Woody's passion for Apollo. Splashdown was scheduled for 2:25 on a Tuesday afternoon, right in the middle of P.E., just like the moon landing. Capitalizing on precedent, the solution was obvious—cut gym once more.

He faked another headache, tricked Martha into another aspirin, and plopped down in front of the TV.

He quivered with excitement and listened to the announcer describe the milestones in somber tones.

"Retro-rockets are firing."

"Entering communications blackout."

"We have a visual. Drogue chute deployed."

"Ten thousand feet. All is go."

"Splashdown! Stable one condition."

A massive lump rose in Woody's throat and a tear trickled down his cheek. *Spectacular. It's a wonder what scientists and engineers can do.* He sniffled and blew his nose. *They say it will be at least five years before the Space Shuttle flies. It's like giving up food for five years.*

Because he'd skipped class again to watch the splashdown, principal Evans called Woody into the office. "Everything at home okay? You've missed a couple of afternoons."

"Sure. Great. Had a tummy bug or something."

* * *

The holidays crept by with no word from Woody's mother except a curious Christmas card that lacked a return address. Woody's days seemed bleak without her. Martha, once a nanny but promoted to a maid because of Woody's age, insisted on a Christmas tree in spite of his father's disinterest. Perpetual Christmas carols on radio and TV, and the lack of presents under the tree depressed Woody nearly to tears.

The first week of January a major snowstorm blanketed the town and Trelor Academy closed, further postponing Woody's Apollo speech. He spent the time aching for his mother and practicing his presentation.

"The roads are finally plowed," announced Woody's father. "I'm going into work. Trelor is open. Martha can drive you to school."

Woody expected the science teacher would finally let him do his talk, so he gathered up his model and index card notes and followed Martha to the car. As they approached the parking lot, Woody's eye began to flutter in excitement about his tale of the launch. With a confident stride, he walked past The King who, he'd heard, had been held back a year. *The dummy is missing rockets. Missing life.*

His first stop was science class where he persuaded Doctor Edwards to let him do his Apollo presentation later that day. After an interminable English class and a boring U.S. history lecture, he strode into the science room clutching the miniature Apollo. Following a go-ahead from Doctor Edwards, Woody trotted to the front of the class and began.

Excitedly, he said, "The whole sky lit up—it was at night, you know. It lifted off but the sound didn't come until a few seconds later. A roar. It almost blew my ears off! When it got high, it turned into a bright star. I watched it until it went away over the horizon." Woody flaunted facts he gleaned from pamphlets he'd picked up saying, "Can you imagine six million pounds going 17,000 miles an hour?" Pointing to his model, he said, "Up top is the command module where the astronauts are. This is the lunar excursion module that landed the guys on the moon. Here's the first, second, and third rocket stages. Now, about the rover…"

His audience became rapt as Woody paced back and forth energetically waving his arms. "It landed on the moon just as planned. The splashdown was exactly on target—after a round trip of half a million miles! Guess we're going to have to wait for that new Space Shuttle before anything like this happens again. Years away. Bummer." He crossed his arms and stared at the kids. "One thing for sure, I'm going to be an astronaut." The whole class clapped. Paul and Larry, his scientific buddies, jumped to their feet cheering. "Count us in!"

After the glory of his speech, the boring routine of school set in. The end of the Apollo program left Woody and his friends feeling empty. Moreover, the chaos of the holidays had vanished leaving exhaustion and ossified minds. No matter how hard they tried, he and his friends couldn't come up with any kind of exciting project. Adrift, Woody simply moped around the house week after week.

* * *

At the end of January, Woody noticed a wayward issue of Popular Science magazine on the teacher's desk. The cover featured an image of the proposed Space Shuttle, and after a heartfelt appeal, Doctor Edwards let him take the magazine home. Thus began a new heroic adventure.

The Herald American
Wednesday, January 17, 1973
Section D1: Entertainment

Jim Croce Tour a Hit

Bad, Bad Leroy Brown Still Topping the Charts

"Hey Woody! You gotta come over and listen to my new record. It's Three Dog Night and their super song Shambala!" shouted Paul. "Got a Croce record too. Totally groovy!"

"I don't have time, my man. I'm working on an out-of-sight model of the new Space Shuttle."

The King strutted up, shouldering his way in front of Woody. "A stupid model, pee-wee? That's for second-graders. You're too dumb to get down on Croce. Surprised your nerdy friend grooves." He smirked and fainted a punch.

Frightened, Woody said, "I have things to do." He turned and rapidly walked toward the bike racks.

Back home, Woody examined his desk with a critical eye. *What a mess! This will never work as a Space Shuttle factory.* He gathered up two old model airplanes, jars of caked paint, a leftover potato chip bag, and an immense assortment of boy-trash. After clearing off a large area on the desk, he went to the garage and liberated a large cardboard box. Back in his room, Woody carefully cut the cardboard to fit the desktop, taking care to cover up the smudges from the matchstick rockets. He stepped back, surveyed the results of his work, and grinned. *Mom would be amazed to see my desk this clean and neat. I wish I could write her a note about my new project.* He rocked back and conjured an image of his mother in his mind. An ache rose in his chest and tears crowded in the corner of his eyes. *She hasn't called but at least she sent a card for Christmas. Odd, there wasn't any return address.*

At that moment he heard his father come in the front door, his work for the day finished. Woody abruptly pushed back from his desk, steeled his resolve, and went to see him. He found him in the kitchen pouring a glass of Jack Daniels with a newspaper tucked under one arm.

"I have to talk with you."

"I need to relax for a while. Maybe later."

"What happened to mom?"

"What happened? I have no idea. Maybe she got tired of living with us." He settled into his easy chair and opened the newspaper.

"Talk to me, father!" Woody cried. "What happened to mom?"

Startled by his son's tone, Woodrow Jr. dropped the paper onto his lap. "What's going on with you?"

"I want to see my mother. Why can't I go visit my mother?"

A look of impatience mixed with sadness covered Woodrow's face. "I understand your desire to see her and wish we could jump into the car and go, but we can't"

"Why not?" Woody demanded.

"Because I don't know where she is. No phone number. No address. No nothing."

"She's gone?" Woody whimpered.

A nod. "Afraid so. I can see that the holidays were tough on you without her."

* * *

"Why are you so sad, Woody?" Martha asked. "Seems you've been in the dumps all week."

He stared at the floor. "I miss Mom, but Father doesn't know where she is. I'd give up my bike if I could go see her."

"Ah—might have guessed. I miss her too and all I can do is wait to see what the future will bring."

"She doesn't care about me. It's not fair!"

"I'm sure you're wrong. Let me ask you a question. Would your mother be happy if she knew you were this depressed mess I've been looking at all week?"

"Guess not."

"Well, young man, I suggest you start behaving like she was about to walk through the door any second." She patted his shoulder and said, "I'm sure she loves you and misses you terribly. With that in mind, why don't you run along and work on that new model you've been talking about."

After Woody had shuffled off to his room, Martha sighed and waddled to her bedroom. She eased her bulk into the rocking chair, crossed her arms, and pondered. *I been with Woody all his life—*

thirteen years now, and he always amazes me. I've never seen such an imagination as his. Then again, he has a knack of getting into trouble. I remember his matchstick rockets. She grinned at the memory. *Guess that was the beginning of his thing for rocket ships. He's at a tough age – puberty and all that. There will be girls soon and I'll bet his father won't even try to give advice to Woody on the biggest mystery he'll ever face. The boy is a treasure. He deserves a mother. Until Helen comes back, I'll do the best I can to help him along.*

It took two days for Martha's advice to sink in. It was late January when Woody said to himself, *Mom would have really liked my model of the Apollo, but she'd be blown away by my Space Shuttle when I finish it.*

* * *

The next day after school, Woody secretly dedicated the Space Shuttle model by naming it after his mother and began work. First, he labored with off-the-cuff speculation and head scratching followed by crude sketches resembling the magazine illustration. A bike trip in bitter cold weather to the nearby hobby shop for a serious talk with the owner brought flashes of insight. The next few afternoons saw detailed sketches illustrating a variety of intricate parts. A list of needed materials appeared: balsawood of various thicknesses, glue, three colors of paint, decals, new Exacto blades, sandpaper, and emery boards.

Woody's father, reveling in quiet evening solitude, wondered where his son was. *It's not like him to disappear every night.* Pleased, he buried himself in the evening newspaper.

The following day, Woody ignored his homework and rummaged through his sock drawer where he'd hid cash from his allowance earmarked for a Christmas present for his mother. He jumped on his bike and soon returned with an armload of hobby store stuff. With deliberate motions, Woody precisely arranged the supplies on the "factory floor." *Good, it begins.*

After a silent dinner with his father, he eagerly took his place in "the factory." *The center fuel tank is the easiest, so I'll start with that. By the time I get to the shuttle itself, I'll be much better.* He sorted through the sheaf of drawings he'd made and pulled out a large sheet. After cutting out the pattern with scissors, he taped it to a piece of balsawood. Carefully, very carefully, he began to cut out the piece with his Exacto knife. Soon, it was eleven at night when his father walked in and exclaimed, "What in the world are you doing at this hour?"

"Just a new model I'm working on."

"Is it a kit? I don't remember buying you one. Looks complicated."

"No. It's my own design. Space Shuttle."

"Whatever. It's late. Get some sleep."

"Sure, in a minute."

Another two hours passed before Woody finally turned in.

A week passed without any word from his mother and the days seemed hollow and gray to Woody. His father tried to put on a show of laughter and cheer, but it rang with insincerity. A big new legal case materialized early February, taking all of his father's attention. In the void, Woody defaulted to the Space Shuttle model—cutting, shaping, sanding, and painting all hours of the day.

This is for you, Mom. Come see it. Painted gleaming white, the main fuel tank took shape.

Nearly three feet tall, its only notable feature was a pipe running its length and a structure where the shuttle proper would be attached. Admiring his work, Woody reverently set it onto a special stand he'd made for it. *Bet this will be what the real one will look like on the launch pad.* He drew up to his full height and solemnly announced: *Woodrow Sterling Lawrence the Third, I promise I will fly in the shuttle. I also promise I will take this model to school and show everyone how mind-blowing it is. I will show them how great our space program is, how humans can live in space, on Mars, on faraway galaxies.*

As the term progressed, homework increasingly encroached on Woody's days and the time he could spend on the model shrank. Paul and Larry ran up to him shouting about their latest ideas and wondering what new schemes Woody had thought up.

"Guys," he said, "I'm working on a mega-hot project at home. I don't have time for anything else. Sorry."

"Aw come on," moaned Larry. "We were talking about that big catapult, right? We were gonna throw snowballs a hundred feet—maybe more. You can't bail out on us."

"No way. This isn't a kid thing like snowballs. It's serious stuff. Real science. It's gonna take two, maybe three weeks to finish. When you guys see it, you'll be blown away."

Except when Martha drove him on snowy days, every afternoon Woody flew home on his bike to work on his shuttle. Larry gave up and treated Woody like a stranger. Paul kept hanging around asking about the project. "Can I come see it? Huh?"

"Naw, no time. Besides, I gotta go see an eye doctor this afternoon. My English teacher noticed I couldn't read the words on the blackboard very well. Called my father. A real bummer."

"A lot of kids have glasses, Woody," Martha said as she drove him to the optometrist. "I'll help you pick out the frames if you like. You may not even need the things, so relax."

A week later, he donned his "dorky glasses" and gasped. "I can read the street signs! I bet I can see better when I work on my Space Shuttle!"

Before long, the two solid rocket boosters, simple cylinders like the main fuel tank, took their position on the display stand. But the shuttle itself, the funny looking airplane, was another matter. Odd compound curves and intricate details presented serious modeling challenges. Woody gritted his teeth and dove in, squinting through his new eyeglasses. Two more weeks passed and the shuttle started to take shape. Paul bugged him constantly to come and see it, but Woody held firm. One afternoon, racing home from school while light snow flurries pelted his face, inspiration struck! *The cargo bay! It should open! That would be cool! I know – I'll put a satellite inside! That'll turn a few heads!* He rubbed his twitching eye.

Another three weeks passed and Paul had given up on him altogether. Larry still wasn't speaking. Oddly, Woody's father started coming around late at night. "That's some kind of rocket," he muttered. "I had no idea it would be so big."

After eleven weeks, Woody slipped a decal of the American flag from the bowl of water and gingerly placed it on the wing of the shuttle. He blotted the excess water with a tissue and rocked back in his chair. *Done at last!*

On a balmy April Tuesday, Martha called the school and made arrangements to deliver the model directly to the science classroom before school actually began. After building a special box big enough to hold the four-foot-long model, Woody struggled to sleep. In the morning, he gingerly jockeyed the packed model in the trunk and clambered into the car. It seemed to Woody that they hit every red light and traffic blocked every street. Eventually Martha pulled into the parking lot where they removed the model and presented it to the waiting teacher.

"Can we open it now?" asked Doctor Edwards.

"No way!" Woody bellowed. "I want to unwrap it during our regular class."

Martha shrugged apologetically.

"Okay. Let's set it over here on the counter," suggested Edwards.

Jittery all morning, Woody rehearsed in his mind exactly what he'd say when he unveiled the model. *Ladies and gentlemen – no, that sounds too stuffy.*

This is the shape of our future space travel. Not bad. How about…

At last, ten o'clock! Woody bolted through the door and stood beside his prize, erect like an Army general. Not knowing what was to come, classmates found their seats, laughing and shouting.

"Settle down, settle down," shouted Doctor Edwards. "We have a special treat for you." Slowly the din faded. "You all know that Woody is an expert on space travel."

A snicker ran through the room.

"Woody has a surprise to show us. I haven't seen it either, but judging from the size of the carton," he went on pointing at Woody and the box, "it has to be impressive. The floor is yours, Woody."

He carried the box to the head of the class and briefly closed his eyes. *This is for you, Mom. Wish you were here.* "Before I open my box, I want to say something about this new space ship that President Nixon announced a while back. Imagine that you step into an airplane and they blast you into orbit. Then your airplane parks next to a fancy workshop and science lab a couple of hundred miles up. You float from your plane into the lab—you float because there isn't any gravity in space. When your job is finished, you climb back into the airplane, come down, and land at the airport. Cool, huh?"

A chorus rang out. "Yeah!" Many students leaned forward in their seats.

The class skeptic called out, "What's the big deal? Croce is something that matters, not stupid space stuff. Who cares about rockets that go nowhere?"

Chuckles.

"Well guys, we're going to do it because it's important. A flying lab like I talked about is supposed to go up in a few weeks. It's called Skylab. Soon we'll be going to Mars, then Jupiter, and maybe even new galaxies someday. Maybe one of you will be the first person on another planet. Maybe me. Cool, huh?"

Pandemonium broke out.

"No way!"

"Really? For sure?"

"Mars? Why not? Been to the moon already."

Woody waved his arms and everyone quieted. "Now for the big moment. You ready?"

"Yessss!"

Slowly, deliberately, Woody removed his model from the box, unwrapping newspaper cushioning, fearful he'd drop the huge thing. He set the display stand on the teacher's desk then positioned the shuttle assembly. Gasps of astonishment greeted him.

"This is a model of how the Space Shuttle could look." Pointing, he went on. "This part is the airplane. It kinda looks like an airplane, doesn't it? This is the main fuel tank. It's as high as a fifteen-story building! Here is the…"

Woody was astonished how soon the school bell rang announcing the end of class. The room broke out in applause and everyone crowded around ogling the model. Both Larry and Paul shouldered alongside gushing accolades, pleasing Woody immensely. As the room emptied, Doctor Edwards came up saying, "You, young man, surpassed any expectation I might have had. Truly spectacular. I have no alternative but to give you an A plus, plus, plus for the day."

Woody basked in the praise.

"I'd like to keep your model here on my desk until tomorrow, okay? I want to show it to my other classes. They'll be amazed."

"Sure. Spread the word. We're goin' to Mars, right?" New thoughts blasted through his head. *Perfect. The more the merrier. Maybe I could talk to his other classes or go to other schools and do my thing.* He threw his shoulders back, thrust his chin out, and rubbed his eye. *I hope Cute Cathy will come see. Maybe I'll ask if she'd like to have a Coke with me.* With that, he swaggered out the door feeling on top of the world.

* * *

Late that afternoon, The King and his posse were jawing in the baseball bleachers after gym. "I'm thinkin' that Led Zeppelin is sooo cool! Grooves, man," The King pronounced. "They've come out with a new album. I'm gonna get it."

"Right on, dude. You see that new gizmo called Atari? Game called Pong? It's far out, man."

A chorus of agreement all around.

"Say, King, you hear about Woody, your bosom buddy?"

"What the fuck you talkin' about? He's nothin' but a four-eyed piece of shit."

"Seems he made a big stir in science class. Showed off a big model he built. Something about a new space ship. The teacher was so impressed he kept the model on his desk to show to his other classes. Wild, man."

"So what?"

"Everybody's talkin' about him. Saying he's another Einstein. He's one hot dude."

The King scowled. "What's the big deal about a crappy model of some sort? Huh? Means nothin' to me."

But it did.

Fuckin' smartass, that's what he is. Always showin' off. Thinks he's so damn smart with his crappy rockets here at the ball diamond and now some kinda model. Everybody talkin' like he's a goddamn genius. Well, maybe I ain't no genius but I'm a hard-nose. When the goddamned school flunked me because that shit-head caught me cheating, I decided I'm gonna live up to my name – King. That's me – The King! It's time that fucking squealer got his.

The schoolyard was emptying fast and The King moseyed over toward the science classrooms. Strolling down the hall, he glanced back and forth making sure no one was in sight. *Gonna check out this fuckin' space ship.*

He paused by the science room door, looked up and down the hall again, and then peeked in through the window. *Nobody in there.* He twisted the knob and surprisingly, the door opened. Quickly, he slipped in.

The first thing that caught his eye was Woody's model. The King walked over and stood in front of it. He spread his feet in a combative stance and hooked his thumbs in his pants pockets. He studied it for a long time with a smirk on his face. Slowly he turned, looked at the door, and seeing no one, The King casually swept his arm and knocked the model off the desk. There was a soft crunching sound as he deliberately set his foot on the delicate balsawood rocket and ground it into the floor.

Let's see what the little shit says about that. He quickly slipped through the door and strutted away.

*   *   *

The next morning dawned bright and clear with a chilly breeze rustling the trees. His jacket warding off the springtime chill, Woody joyfully drank in the crisp air as he pedaled to school. His thoughts reached out to a majestic time where the model would inspire more kids, and how Cute Cathy would be impressed with the amazing depiction of future space travel. *First thing, I'll ask Doctor Edwards if I can talk to all his classes like I did yesterday. Other public schools and…* He pumped his bike faster.

Bursting with energy, he ran to the science room and dashed through the door where he saw Doctor Edwards staring at the floor. Woody's eyes followed the teacher's gaze to the pulverized balsawood remnants of his model. Stunned, Woody knelt and tenderly touched one piece, then another. Turning to Doctor Edwards, he stammered, "What? How?"

"I don't know. It was this way when I got here."

Woody choked back tears as he picked up a small chunk of the shuttle. "Why would anybody want to..." Tears dripped on his glasses while he gasped. "I know who'd do this. Yes, it has to be him!"

"Who?" the teacher asked.

"The King, that's who. He's had it out for me for a long, long time."

"Are you sure? How do you know?"

"I just do. No doubt." He gulped. "Gotta report this to Principal Evans. Right now!" His hands shaking, Woody scraped the scattered pieces into a pile and began putting them into the box he'd brought. "I hate him! Hate him!"

Racked with anger, Woody drew curious glances from students as he stumbled to the principal's office, Doctor Edwards following closely. He rushed past the secretary who called out, "Hey, you can't barge in there!"

Oblivious, Woody halted in front of the principal, held out the box of debris, and stammered, "The King did this. You gotta find him; punish him!" His choking and gasping stopped further words.

Principal Evans raised a quizzical eyebrow toward Doctor Edwards. "What's all this about?"

"Woody built a beautiful model of the proposed Space Shuttle and…" The teacher went on to explain the details, how they conformed to the magazine illustration, and the exceptional presentation Woody made. "Then I found it like this on the floor this morning."

"It took me almost three months to build," screamed Woody.

"Easy, easy, young man," soothed Principal Evans. "You say The King did this? You mean Harold Kingster?"

"That's him, for sure. You gotta tell his parents! The cops too!"

"Perhaps. Did you actually see Kingster do it?"

Woody wiped his nose on his sleeve. "No, but I know he did it."

"How about you, Doc. See anything?"

"No, I didn't. I got caught up in a meeting last night, so I locked up later than usual; but I didn't go into the classroom. I found Woody's model on the floor when I opened up this morning. No sign of anybody."

"I *know* The King did it," Woody whimpered.

Principal Evans nodded with sympathy. "Tell you what, let me talk to Kingster. See what I can find out. Come see me tomorrow afternoon, okay?"

Shoulders sagging, Woody crept out of the office clutching the fragments. He chucked the whole box into a trashcan and rode his bike back home, teetering in agony.

* * *

Martha greeted the older Woodrow at the door. "Something is wrong with your son, Mr. Lawrence. He came home around eleven this morning, very upset. Went straight to his room and wouldn't talk to me."

"What now?" Woodrow grumbled in disgust.

"I tried to talk with him—see if I could help, but he wouldn't come out."

"Great. I lost a big trial today and come home to drama. Guess I'll see what his problem is." He found Woody face down on the bed, the pillow over his head. Woodrow sat on the edge of the bed and tapped Woody's shoulder. "Hey, what's going on?"

A muffled "Nothin'," crept from beneath the pillow.

"Looks like something to me. Come on; tell me about it." Getting no response, Woodrow tugged the pillow away and pulled his son upright. Shocked by Woody's tear-stained cheeks and runny nose, he took Woody's shoulders and looked him straight in the eye. "Come on, son. Give."

Tears started flowing again. "The King busted up my model."

"What? Your new big replica of the Space Shuttle?"

All Woody could manage was to nod.

"The King? The King at school?"

Another nod.

"Did you tell a teacher? The principal?"

Yet another nod.

"What are they going to do?"

"Nothin'."

"What do you mean, nothing?"

"Maybe they'll talk to The King. Don't remember." In halting breaths, Woody explained that nobody actually saw The King bust up the model.

That nobody believed him that it was The King. "But I'm positive," he whimpered.

"Did you confront this King guy himself? What did he say?"

Woody shrugged and looked down at the floor.

"Losing your space ship is terrible, I get it. But you can't accuse people without proof. You've got to meet with this King fellow and confront him. Ask around to find out what other kids know. If you can prove to me that this King did it, I'll call Principal Evans and resolve all this. But I can't move until you show me proof. Understand?"

"I can't. I can't go back to school."

"You must and you will. No more nonsense." Woodrow rose and stalked from the room.

Woody began crying again. *Talk to The King? He'll pound me. I can't ask around; everybody is too scared of The King to say anything bad about him. There's just no way.*

* * *

After a sleepless night, Woody staggered from bed and took his place at the table where Martha presented him with eggs and bacon, which turned his stomach. "Father's gone to work already?"

Martha nodded. "About half an hour ago. You feeling better?"

Woody pushed his eggs away. "Nope."

The chair squealed against the floor as Martha drew it up next to Woody. She patted his arm saying, "Your father is busy preparing an appeal for that big case he lost yesterday, so he hasn't time to help you. Let me try, okay?"

"No use."

"You never know. Just tell me what's going on. Just saying it might help."

Her warm smile and kind eyes caressed him, smothering Woody's resistance. "It's my model of the Space Shuttle. It's gone."

"Gone? What do you mean?"

"The King smashed it but I can't prove it. Nobody saw him do it."

"The King? The bully at school you always talk about?"

"Yeah. He smashed it into pieces." Woody went on to tell the whole tale like barging into the principal's office—everything.

"I imagine your father is in a rage. What did he say when you told him last night?"

"Said I had no proof. Said I should walk up to The King and make him admit it."

Martha re-arranged her bulk in the chair and said, "You want to do that?"

"No! He'll pound me into the ground!"

"Any other ideas?"

"No."

"Seems to me that a teenaged fellow like yourself might think about confronting his problems straightaway. You're letting that thug run your life. That what you want?"

Her words bit into Woody's brain and he shuddered. "It's not fair! It took months to build that model! He had no right to smash it!"

"So?"

"I gotta get him to admit it!"

"You'll need witnesses I'm thinking."

Woody's eye began to twitch and he hitched himself tall in the chair. "Maybe..."

Martha grinned. "Are you thinking 'a pounding' might be a small price to nail The King. You have a plan?"

"It's coming to me."

* * *

That morning's science class was a disaster. The other kids pretended they knew nothing about the disaster. The silence penetrated Woody's skull and scrambled his thoughts. Even Paul and Larry were too embarrassed to speak, but at the end of class he cornered them anyway.

"Wait up, guys. I need your help."

Woody's friends stuck their hands into the pockets of their Jeans and stared at the floor. "What kind of help?"

"I'm positive The King trashed my model; I just don't have proof."

"He's the kind of jerk who would," Larry said, shifting his feet.

"Here's my plan. At lunch I'm gonna walk right up to him in the quad and accuse him face-to-face. Get him to admit it."

Paul blanched. "Man, he'll kill you. Want us to arrange for your funeral?"

"I don't know what else to do," Woody said with a hollow chuckle. "I might have to get him real mad before he comes clean, but whatever it takes."

"You're nuts," Larry exclaimed.

"Probably. Here's what I need from you two. You go with me to the quad and listen carefully to what The King says. My father says I need witnesses and that's your job. After he admits he smashed my model, you guys can go with me to the principal's office and prove I'm right. Deal?"

"Hah! You're nuts. But I always did like watching a fight," Larry said. "I'm in."

"Me too."

But the plans he'd put together made him nauseous. Deliberate steps took him to the quad with Larry and Paul trailing behind, trying to look disinterested. There, Woody spotted The King chumming with his posse. Summoning what courage he could, he walked up to his nemesis. "King, why did you bust up my model rocket last night?"

"What are you talkin' about, four eyes? I didn't bust anything, but I'm thinkin' I should bust your face for interrupting me and my boys." The King pointedly flexed his biceps.

Woody almost peed his pants. "You broke it. Just admit you broke it."

The King roared with laughter. He turned to his friends saying, "Hear that guys? This tiny turd wants me to take the blame for whatever happened to some kind of stupid model."

The others laughed too. The King stood face-to-face with Woody and hissed, "Get lost, little shit."

Woody glanced over his shoulder and confirmed that Larry and Paul were watching the scene intently. Moreover, a number of other kids crowded in hoping to see a brawl. He turned back to face The King and sucked in a halting breath. "You did it; I know you did it. You don't have the balls to admit it. Your guys are always saving you. Without them you're just a punk. You cheat on tests and flunked a grade. You're nothing!"

The King reached out and grabbed Woody's collar screaming, "And you're nothing but a fucking tattletale. You think that bitchy model made you hot shit!" He yanked hard on Woody's collar. "Hell yes!" he roared. "I knocked it off the desk and ground it into the floor!"

Fear choked off Woody's breath and his face turned white. "There, you admit it," he stammered. "You smashed my Space Shuttle!"

The King cocked his arm. "Damn right, and I'm gonna smash your face!" With that, he slugged Woody on the nose drawing a spurt of blood and knocking his eyeglass to the pavement. "Miserable piece of shit!" Before Woody could recover and protect himself, a wild right hand hit him on the cheek, knocking him to the ground. The posse applauded and when The King moved in to kick the prone figure, a burly arm suddenly curled around his throat. Howie, the school janitor, yanked the assailant aside and threw him against a picnic table. "Enough!" he growled. Dazed, The King fell to pavement and Howie straddled him, preventing escape.

Within moments, teachers and office staff arrived and carted The King off to the principal. Others lifted Woody from the ground and blotted blood from his nose. Paul shouldered into the crowd and rescued Woody's broken glasses.

An hour later, Woody found himself in Doctor Edwards' car, headed home. The teacher lightly poked Woody's shoulder. "Well done," he said.

* * *

"Oh, my God!" Martha cried when Doctor Edwards ushered Woody into the house. "What happened?"

"First, let me introduce myself. I'm Doctor Edwards, Woody's science teacher. Seems like Woody had a 'discussion' with a kid at school. A big kid, I might add."

In near hysterics, Martha sat Woody in a chair and fled down the hall for first-aid supplies. "Oh my, oh my," she wailed.

Woody tried not to flinch as Martha dabbed mercurochrome on his split lip and gently pinched his nose to stop the bleeding. Doctor Edwards took his leave saying, "Things look under control. See you in class, Woody."

With skill, Martha nursed her patient. "There, that should do fine. I don't think you need to see a doctor, but we'll see what your father says. I'll call him right now and let him know what happened." She gathered up the bloody tissues and studied her patient's face. "Are you smiling? Why are you smiling?"

Woody's grin spread as far as his split lip allowed. "I did it."

"Did what?"

"I made The King admit he trashed my model. Picked a fight with him. I had witnesses this time."

"Oh my goodness; you father will be thrilled! I can't believe you'd do a thing like that. You've always been so.....studious.

* * *

Woodrow burst into the house and rushed to where his son was sitting. "Holy mackerel, you look like a truck ran over you. You okay?"

"I'll be fine, Father. No big deal."

"No big deal? Your lip is bigger than a sausage and you'll have a beaut of a shiner. You hurt bad anywhere?"

"Naw. Actually, I think of my black eye as a badge of honor," he beamed.

"Are you crazy? Who did this to you?"

Martha patted Woody's head. "Tell him all the glorious details, Woody. This afternoon was a hallmark in your life."

Woodrow leaned forward in anticipation, forgetting to correct Martha's use of Woody for his son's name. "Tell me what happened."

Erect in his chair, Woody explained everything. How he taunted The King, how he stood his ground, how he'd arranged for witnesses.

Stunned, Woodrow could only shake his head. Finally, he managed, "I never imagined. What got into you?"

"Just did what you suggested father. Now I can go to the principal and prove that The King totaled my model. I hope to get him expelled. Better yet, thrown in jail."

Martha leaned back, crossed her arms, and said, "It looks like Woody grabbed life by the throat today. I'm proud of him."

Woodrow reached over and put his hand on Woody's shoulder. "So am I."

A bit of a tear sparkled in the corner of Woody's good eye. "I'll need a ride to school tomorrow, Martha. Can't see so good without my glasses. Okay?"

"No, not okay!" shouted Woodrow "I'll take him myself and speak to the principal first thing. I'll call the school right now and make arrangements. I need the names of your friends who were 'witnesses.' You said the janitor broke up the fight? Need him too. The King, of course and whoever handles security on campus." Woodrow grinned and rubbed his hands. "This is going to be a show!"

* * *

The next morning at the breakfast table Woody could hardly swallow from excitement and a sore jaw. Woodrow confirmed that the principal and all the others would meet them at nine that morning. As his father drove them to school, Woody mentally rehearsed what he wanted to say and asked his father for advice from time to time.

Woodrow turned into a visitor's parking slot and followed Woody toward the administrative offices. Together, they strode up to the receptionist. "Woodrow Lawrence to see Principal Evans."

With an officious scowl, the middle-age woman tipped her head toward an open door and said, "Go on in; everyone is expecting you."

With determined steps, Woodrow entered the office and shook the principal's hand while Woody took a seat in a vacant chair. He looked around and saw Larry and Paul grinning widely. Conversely, The King scowled, arms crossed and jaw clenched. Woody nodded to the vice principal responsible for campus discipline. Principal Evans' secretary hovered close-by, notepad in hand.

"This is a very serious matter," Principal Evans began. "Mister Kingster is accused of fighting on campus and of vandalism. First, let's talk about yesterday's fight. Mister Kingster, what is your version? Did you strike Woody Lawrence?"

"He hit me first."

"Bull," uttered Larry.

"Please, everyone. Let's keep order. Please remember, Mister Kingster, we have witnesses to corroborate your testimony."

The King leaned forward in his chair and growled, "He was bad-mouthin' me. Calling me names."

"Please answer the question. Did you hit him?" With an exaggerated motion, Principal Evans stared at Woody's bandage and black eye. "Did you?"

The King shrugged.

"I'll take that as a yes. Did Mister Lawrence strike you? I see no injuries."

"Well..." The King squirmed in his chair. "He was going to."

Larry slapped his forehead with a loud smack.

"You certain?" queried Principal Evans. "We have people who were there."

The King glared at Larry and Paul and received smiles in return. "Well, I thought he would."

"Mister Edelstein, what did you see?"

"Just call me Howie; I'm only the janitor you know. Kingster slugged him good—knocked him on the ground. Went to kick him, but I grabbed him first."

Larry and Paul nodded vigorously.

"Comments Mister Kingster?"

"Don't remember."

"Thank you, Mister Edelstein. That will be all for now. You're excused. Larry Gray and Paul Middleton, you saw everything?"

"Sure did," they replied in unison.

Principal Evans spun a pencil on his desktop. "To your knowledge, is everything you've heard true?"

"Darn right."

"Spot on."

"Woody Lawrence, do you wish to add anything?"

"It's true I wanted to bait The King. I wanted to get him so mad that he'd admit smashing my model of the Space Shuttle." Woody touched his bruised cheek. "Guess he got mad, alright."

"At any time did you threaten to punch him?"

"No, sir."

Evans tilted his head to his secretary. "Okay, let's move on to this model you spoke of. Tell me about it."

"It was…" Woody tried not to choke up.

Woodrow spoke up. "Because Doctor Edwards, Woody's science teacher, is in class at the moment, he gave me a note for you. He describes the model in detail, confirming it was very elaborate."

Woody tried to pull himself together. "Wasn't a kit. My own, from a magazine picture. Took months."

Evans rubbed his chin thoughtfully. "Mister Kingster. Did you admit you broke the model?"

"No way!" The King bellowed.

Woody gasped and Larry jerked to his feet.

"Be careful, Mister Kingster. I believe we can assemble a large number of witnesses." He turned to Larry and Paul. "Gentlemen, did you hear Mister Kingster admit he smashed Mister Lawrence's model?"

"Yes, sir!"

"Absolutely!"

"Well, everyone," Evans concluded. "I believe we have all the pertinent information at hand. Mister Kingster did in fact strike a fellow student and also destroyed a prized possession of the same student. The Trelor Academy will now take appropriate steps."

Woodrow rose to his feet. "As a local attorney, I plan to bring suit against this Kingster and his family. I would appreciate the cooperation of the Trelor academy in assembling my case. I'm also interested in specific steps the school will take to prevent bullying. Please keep me informed."

Principal Evans rose and shook hands with Woodrow. "We'll see what we can do Mister Lawrence, but we'll have to be somewhat careful about precedent and the reputation of our school. Our teenage boys are at an awkward age and tend toward aggression."

* * *

That afternoon during lunch, Larry and Paul slapped Woody on the back. "You thumped his butt!

Expelled! The whole school appreciates what you've done!"

Woody snuck a peek at King's posse grousing across the way, flashing harsh stares at him. "I'm not sure that *everyone* would agree," he muttered nervously.

Paul wagged a finger under Woody's nose. "If you want to put the final screws to The King, you should build your Space Shuttle again."

"Yeah," cried Larry. "You could do those talks to Doctor Edwards' other classes like you talked about. You'd be a hero!"

"He already is a hero," Cute Cathy said, walking over. She stared at Woody's bandage and black eye. "Does it hurt much?"

"Not much." Woody grimaced as a big smile pulled at his split lip. "In a few days you'd never know what happened." His heart thumped so hard he worried Cute Cathy would see his shirt flutter.

"I think Paul has a wonderful idea," she said. "Build another model. Everyone says your first one was spectacular."

"I suppose I could. It would take months though." *But still, talking to all of Doctor Edwards' classes or even showing my stuff at other schools would be incredibly cool.*

At that moment the posse swaggered past tossing mean glances and flexing muscles. *But then again, it might be another one of my big fancy schemes gone bad. Sometimes it seems that my brain is at war with me.*

The Herald American
Thursday, April 5, 1973
Section C1: Technology Today

Pioneer 11 on its Way
Will Visit Asteroid Belt, Saturn, and Jupiter

Woody lost all interest in space since Apollo had folded and paid no attention to Pioneer 11. *It's not like walking on the moon.* He thought of Cute Cathy and searched his mind for the energy to re-build his Space Shuttle model, but he only mumbled, "Maybe I'll start next week."

The days dragged slowly from April into May. His fears became realized as The King's posse found innovative ways to torment him, snatching his eyeglasses or scattering homework papers across the lawn, always out of sight of the school staff. He found the word "shit-head" painted on his locker and Eller, the biggest follower of The King, shouldered Woody into a picnic table at every chance; unseen of course. Bruised, Woody gave up going to the quad after Principal Evans said there was nothing he could do.

As the weather warmed, Woody's energy continued to wane. His grades, once straight A's became C's and D's. Teachers gave Woody notes in sealed envelopes to take to his father, but Woody didn't deliver them. As things worsened, their notes became phone calls to his home, triggering harsh upbraids from his father. Even Cute Cathy found him too depressed to talk to and avoided him. Larry and Paul devised a scheme to customize their skateboards and began entering competitions, ignoring Woody.

By late May, Woody was nearly dysfunctional and had given up any chance to rebuild his model shuttle. When Eller punched him in the kidney, Woody screamed obscenities at him. That afternoon, when Woody went to his bike for the ride home, he found it trashed.

* * *

It was Friday, the last day of the spring term and Woody stared at his report card. English: D, History: D, Science: C-, Math: C-, Phys Ed: F. *What will happen when father sees this? I tried to pull up my grades after The*

King was thrown out, but the posse took over. I'm in big trouble.

Celebrating vacation at the end of the day, hundreds of kids whooped and yelled in joy, running to their rides or the bus. Woody didn't notice.

"Hey Woody, see you in a couple of weeks when the summer session starts up," Larry yelled as he flew past on his skateboard. Woody just clutched the report card, his hand shaking. He was jarred from his trance by a honking horn. Martha waved through the windshield. "Come on!"

He half staggered, half stumbled to the car and got in. "Tomorrow's the big day," bubbled Martha. "Your father asked me to take you shopping for a new bike to replace your damaged one. Maybe a mountain bike like you want."

"Probably not."

"Oh, come on." Martha turned and glanced at Woody. "Something wrong?"

"I'm thinkin' I'm dead."

Is he having still another snit? Martha clenched her jaw and drove home without further words.

That afternoon, Woody lay in his bed covered in sweat when he heard his father stride through the front door and greet Martha. "Hi. How are you doing? Dinner going to be on time?"

Woody heard a thump as Woodrow set down his briefcase. He couldn't hear the sigh when his father dropped into the easy chair and couldn't hear the rustle of the evening newspaper. But he knew his father was hidden behind the pages with his drink. Ten minutes, twenty minutes went by as Woody quaked in the bed. Then he heard, "Martha! Isn't today the last day of school?" There was a murmur. "Right, I thought so. See if you can find my son and bring him to me. Lots to talk about."

He heard creaking steps on the stairs and a soft rap on his door. "Woodrow? You in there?"

"Yes," Woody stammered.

"Your father would like to speak to you. Maybe about the bike?"

"Be right down." He went to the bathroom and wiped his face with a cold washcloth. With a gulp, Woody picked up the report card and went to face his father.

"Ah, there you are. Ready for a nice two-week vacation?"

Rigid, Woody held out the card. "Here."

"Oh, right." Woodrow reached out, took it, and briefly scanned it. Slowly his face turned red and his jaw muscles bulged. He adjusted his glasses and peered intently. "What…is…this?"

Woody managed to shrug.

"Well?" roared Woodrow.

His knees shaking, Woody sputtered "Well, you know, it was the King thing."

"What does that have to do with anything? The thug was expelled. In juvie the last I heard."

"It's not just The King. All his sidekicks kept tormenting me. I mentioned that to you a couple of times."

"Look, I called that Evans guy about that and he assured me he'd take care of it the best he can. So how does that explain this?" He slapped the report card.

"There's more. I…I hoped to build another Space Shuttle and show it to all the other classes Doctor Edwards taught. I wanted to talk about the glory of space travel." Tearful eyes glittered behind his glasses. "I wanted to explain to the kids how science is wonderful. I thought about taking the model to other schools and show them about..."

"Good grief! Another of your wild schemes! I should have paid more attention to those telephone calls from your teachers. You know what you've done, don't you? You've compromised your chances to get into Yale Law School!" He threw the report card on the floor. "I don't know what I'm going to do with you."

Needless to say, there was no shopping trip for a mountain bike. Grounded. No TV. His father demanded he study English and history with Martha, read *The Meditations by Marcus Aurelius,* write an essay on the importance of college...

A week later Woody's father informed him he wouldn't be returning to "that weak-kneed Trelor school," but instead he'd attend the LeMay Military Academy known for merciless discipline.

The Herald American
Thursday, September 11, 1977
Section D1: Business Section

New Computer Game Introduced

Atari Promises to Capitalize on New Personal Computer Craze

"Yer left, yer left, yer left, right left," barked the drill instructor as Woody sweated profusely in the September sun. *What's the point of close order drill? Totally stupid,* he groused silently.

It had been four years since his father enrolled him in the LeMay Military Academy, a boarding school in Weymouth. Living in a dorm, the need for a bicycle or rides from Marta vanished. The first year had been hell for Woody. Although pleased to be done with The King and his posse, he yearned for rocket talks with Doctor Edwards and chit-chat with Cute Cathy. By the second year, he'd become more accustomed to the stern words from instructors and admonishments to sit and walk like a true military man. Essentially friendless, Woody spent the following year in a melancholy daze, but his zeal for science bloomed once more comforting him.

Entering his senior year, Woody defied his father and signed up for advanced physics and pre-calculus instead of social studies and business education. Memories of The King and Cute Cathy vanished long ago and oddly, he discovered the strict environment at LeMay shoved him toward adulthood and his grades increasingly improved. Gone was the self-doubt, but his wild, out-of-the-box imagination wrapped its arms around Woody and squeezed mightily. Science reigned in his mind; he had no use for art, music, or literature. Consequently, his classmates found him bizarre and banished him to the fringes. He rarely spoke to his father who preferred to check with the administration office directly rather than his son. On top of all that, raging acne repulsed the girls, so Woody settled into the role of a loner, playing Atari for hours on end and reading Scientific American Magazine.

The exception was Bill Butler, a dumpy nerd replete with thick eyeglasses and a pocket saver stuffed with drafting pencils, a six-inch ruler, and a silly little slide rule. Like Woody, Bill came from a wealthy family who largely ignored him. Steeped in science, the two bonded and indulged in Einstein, black hole speculation, and Rube Goldberg contraptions. Their lockers were devoid of baseball mitts or football cleats, but overflowed with textbooks, chemistry glassware, and spent rocket casings.

"Dismissed," bellowed the drill instructor.

Finally, Woody breathed. He dashed to the showers, toweled off, and jumped into his immaculate school uniform, anxious to meet his friend Bill.

"What's happenin', my man?"

"Have you heard about this new company called Apple?" Bill chuckled. "Who'd call a company 'Apple' for cryin' out loud?"

Woody shrugged. "What are you talking about?"

"It's a brand-new computer company. Not big mainframes like IBM, but small ones. They call theirs Apple II."

"So, who cares?"

"What kind of question is that coming from a world-class scientific like yourself?" Bill sputtered.

Woody blushed. "Well, I'm not big into computers, you know, although I've heard about the IBM 370. What makes this one so special?"

"Let's find out! I talked to Colonel Gould in the lab. He knows a lot about Apple because the school just bought one. It's in the physics lab as I speak!" Bill caught his breath. "He said the company was started by a couple of guys just like us, only they're older—twenty-one. One's called Jobs and the other is Wozniak or something like that. Best of all, Gould said he'd show us how to work the machine. Isn't that cool?"

"It might be fun to fool around with something new. I'm kinda tired of rockets even though the Space Shuttle is finally doing glide tests right now. Didn't go to the moon or anything."

"What are we waiting for? Let's go talk with Gould!"

"I dig it!" shouted Woody. A familiar surge of enthusiasm filled him and a twitch tickled his eyes. *I'll bet these computer things could be as exciting as rockets, though maybe in a quiet way. Although in truth, even Atari is getting boring.*

Four days had passed when a very irritable Colonel Gould grumbled, "I have to teach a few subjects, you know. I don't have hours on end to show you two the ins and outs of this baby computer. Between classes, why don't you come on in and tinker with it on your own. You can't hurt the beast."

So, it began. Woody and Bill became consumed with passion for the typewriter-style keyboard and the Sony monitor, both orchestrated by a small box of electronics. Unknown to Woodrow, his hopes of Yale Law School for his son succumbed to flickering lines of code and excited repartee between the two boys taking big bites from their bizarre Apple. They spent every spare moment in the far corner of the lab, pondering and solemnly discussing fresh ideas. Before long, the Colonel began asking them to explain the more sophisticated aspects of programming.

Woody and Bill were oblivious of the boisterous students who occupied the lab while the Colonel taught his classes. They failed to hear the caustic comments like "What's with those two guys? Looks like they're on a different planet."

In a way they were. Programming wasn't enough. They researched the mainframe computers and read avidly about Jobs and Wozniak. Both were surprised to discover that the Apple II had been developed in Jobs' garage.

"Just a couple of guys like us. No reason we can't do even better," boasted Woody, spreading his arms wide.

No longer a simple interest, programming became their religion and the box of electronics a totem. Wild ideas flew about like a covey of quail flushed by a Labrador retriever. Inevitably, fatigue dampened their speculations, but Bill insisted they "Keep on steppin'." Often, the night watchman evicted them from the lab.

In spite of all the hours spent tickling the Apple, Woody remembered his father's reaction to the bad report card from Trelor, and managed to keep his grades up for the most part. While struggling with an exhaustive problem in his math class, another inspiration came to Woody.

"Bill, I've been fighting this statistics thing and I've spent hours on it. It's not very complex, just a bunch of repetitive calculations. You think our Apple friend could be programmed to help?"

"Of course!"

They dove in. "Maybe we could do a table, kinda like a matrix," Woody suggested. "We could see if it would organize a bunch of numbers."

"But we have to multiply some, add others. How we gonna do that?"

"If we try..."

A week flew by, then another. At times they became so tired they could hardly keep their eyes open while pecking at the keyboard, but somehow their program kept getting better.

"This is way beyond the Colonel and now *we're* even struggling," Bill grumbled. "Should we get someone else's help? Maybe Major Mockli, the calculus instructor?"

"What's to lose?" Woody said. His breath quickened with the thought of bringing better expertise to the project, which could speed things along. He rubbed his twitching eye.

* * *

Major Mockli had no time for off-the-wall schemes. He'd been warned by Colonel Gould that the two kids could drive a saint bonkers with their enthusiasm. Evading a potential problem, he arranged a meeting with two honor students on whom he could pawn off the looming disaster.

Woody swallowed a gasp when he was introduced to the newcomers. One was a tall muscular boy with a trim mustache and a spring in his step like a trained athlete. The other was a girl! She had a bright smile, freckles, and a waistline on the dumpy side.

"Woody, Bill, meet Jose Rodriguez and Peggy Jacob," Mockli said. "They're two of my best students, both well versed in calculus and differential equations."

They shook hands awkwardly. "We're trying to work up a special program for the new computer in the physics lab," Woody explained. "Know about it?"

Jose and Peggy shook their heads. "Didn't know they had one," said Peggy.

Standing, Major Mockli said, "You don't need me. As you kids say, I'm gonna blow this taco stand. It's up to Colonel Gould and you people now." He marched through the door without looking back, leaving the uncomfortable kids staring at one another.

"Now what?" Jose asked.

"Let's get a load off our feet," Bill said, sitting at a desk. The others followed. "Here's the deal," he continued. "Woody and I have been trying to come up with some kind of matrix on that new computer, an Apple II."

Both Jose and Peggy gave blank looks in return. "A matrix to do what?" asked Jose.

Woody cleared his throat. "Maybe not a *real* matrix, but a chart-like thing that could organize a bunch of numbers and do arithmetic like add and divide."

"Why do you need us? We do advanced math, not simple stuff like you're sayin'." Jose said. "Right Peggy?"

"Yeah," Peggy folded her arms. "Besides, neither of us have a clue about computers. I don't see how we could help."

"We're stuck," Woody murmured. "We need fresh eyes on our project. If we can work out some bugs, this machine could be the best thing since chocolate ice cream. This could be the dawn of a new computer age!" His voice rose. "This is our chance to push technology to the stars. I bet it won't be long before everybody has their own computer at home."

"Aw, come on," chuckled Jose. "Been dropping a little acid?"

"I'm not so sure Woody's wrong, Jose," Peggy said. "It wasn't that long ago we didn't have televisions. My grandparents told me that their first phone number was three longs and a short. Now we have mobile phones in cop cars. Things are changing fast."

Jose scowled and waved his hand at Woody and Bill. "You're saying these two brainiacs are on to something as important as television sets?"

With a broad smile, Peggy said, "You never know."

Indignant, Woody wagged his finger at Jose. "Brainiacs, huh? Jobs and Wozniak are brainiacs making miracles in their garage. Invented the funny little computer that's in the physics lab. Bill and I are going down the same path!"

Peggy giggled. "So, Jose, what are you going to do with the rest of your afternoon? Play catch with your buddies? Me, I'm going to look at a funny little computer with these guys." She threaded her hands through Woody's and Bill's arms. "Let's get steppin'."

Jose tried to formulate a snide comment, then said, "Wait up."

They bustled over to the lab and Woody led them to their table in the corner. "This is it!" he said proudly.

In chorus, both Peggy and Jose exclaimed, "That's it? It looks like a typewriter gone nuts."

Ignoring the crack, Bill plopped in the chair and flipped a switch. "Watch this." The monitor glowed and lines of text appeared on the screen.

"Show them our table, Bill," Woody instructed.

As a late October gust of wind whirled outside, Bill tapped on the keyboard and showed Peggy and Jose how programs could be made to do things. The two newcomers pulled up chairs and stared. An hour passed, and then another.

Beaming, Woody said, "We've put together this table filled with numbers which makes it easy to see patterns, but we need more. That's where you two could come in. Dig it?"

"Like a matrix of some sort? Like we were talking about?" asked Peggy.

Woody shrugged. "Whatever."

Halloween came and went, as did Thanksgiving and Christmas. They abandoned plans for a New Year's party. They chafed at time spent on classes and homework and close-order drill. Instructors and students pointed and laughed when they passed by, but the newcomers were sucked into the vortex of Woody's vision and never noticed.

By Valentine's Day, they'd made real progress.

"Check this out," Woody said, trembling. "Using Peggy's idea, we can multiply the number in this square by the number over here. Bingo!"

"If we do this," Jose said reaching over Woody's shoulder and typing, "we can divide too!"

Silence fell over the foursome. They stared at one another and grinned broadly. "That it?"

They broke into boisterous laughter. "We did it! It works!"

Minutes later, the significance of their achievement settled in their thoughts and they quieted.

Bill broke the silence. "Now what?"

Heads shook, shoulders shrugged.

"This is just the beginning," Woody blurted. "Let's show Gould and Mockli what we have. I bet they'll be blown away. Then the next step—we start our own company to sell the program to all the Apple II owners in the world! We could go and meet Jobs and Wozniak, team up with them..."

As predicted, Colonel Gould and Major Mockli were amazed. But as adults cursed with realism, they pointed out that a lot of money would be required to fully polish the program, perform beta testing, do a market survey, and set up production equipment.

Riding a tsunami of excitement, Woody said, "I'm sure we'd consider taking on partners if they had cash. How would you two like to buy in? We'll all be rich!"

Squelching chuckles, Gould and Mockli pointed out they were educators, not business people. Further, as employees of LeMay, they weren't exactly flush with money. "But thanks anyway."

"You'll be sorry," Woody said with a straight face.

As the foursome walked away, Jose said, "They have a point, you know. We're gonna need a lot of money if we want to start a business. How we gonna get it?"

Woody dismissed Jose's words with a wave of his hand. "There's no problem. This idea of ours is so earthshaking, we'll have to fight off mobs of people trying to get rich."

Bill scratched his chin. "Not if nobody knows about it. How do we spread the news?"

"I have an idea," said Peggy. "Let's advertise in the school newspaper, the *LeMay Ledger*. All the kids will tell their parents who'll come running."

"Great," shouted Woody. "Before class tomorrow I'll run over to their office and make arrangements."

The next morning he did, although he had to explain how the computer program was a school sponsored thing and not a commercial endeavor. He felt no qualms telling a white lie; otherwise they wouldn't run an article.

A brief notice appeared in the *Ledger* three days later, but after a week had passed, there were no inquiries. Woody was incredulous. "What's the matter with people? Don't they know they're missing out on a miracle?"

"That might be an exaggeration," Bill pointed out. "No matter, the ad didn't work. So what are we going to do now?"

The question was met with scowls and silence.

Depressed, Woody trudged back to his dorm, flopped on the bed nursing a sudden headache. He skipped dinner, his mind grasping for ways to raise money, for ways to get the word out. Night fell and no solutions appeared.

Midnight.

Two in the morning.

"Of course!" He shouted.

His roommate woke and blurted, "Shut up!"

His mind spinning, Woody thought, *we need horsepower, big horsepower! We'll set up a powwow with Jobs and Wozniak. They'll understand what our program can do. Support us. Why didn't I think of this before?* Then he remembered. He *had* thought of it, but the idea had been washed away by the rush to finish the program.

After class once more, they gathered to compose a letter to Apple Computer. It wasn't a calm meeting with all four offering heated advice and quibbling over wording. They all realized the letter was their last shot at raising money.

"Look," Woody said, "They pick up the mail in an hour. The letter is fine. Let's take it over to the office right away."

"We can buy stamps there," Peggy pointed out. "Too bad we couldn't find a phone number for Apple—lucky enough to have an address."

Two agonizing weeks passed with no word from Apple. Grumbling. Long faces. Lost dreams.

It was Jose who voiced what they all felt. "Guess this idea is goin' nowhere. Kaput. Finished. It was fun while it lasted."

Bill and Peggy shook their heads and stared at the ground. "He's right."

"We can't give up," Woody cried. "Our program will put small computers on the map. We just can't give up!"

"So, where do we go from here?"

"I promised myself not to ask my father for money," Woody mumbled, "but I've no choice now." He took a deep breath. "Bill, your dad's loaded, how about him? Jose? Peggy?"

"I could try," Bill said. "He thinks I've been wasting my time chumming around with you, but I'll give it a go."

Jose laughed. "I'm on scholarship; my folks are dirt poor. No chance."

"Count me out," Peggy said. "I had a huge fight with dad when I decided to major in math instead of nursing or some other ladylike thing. He would *never* consider helping me starting a risky business."

"Crap," muttered Woody. "I guess it's up to you and me, Bill."

* * *

Setting aside his newspaper, Woodrow hissed sarcastically. "Just a few thousand dollars? For some lamebrain scheme about baby computers?"

"Father, you have to listen to me," Woody whimpered. "The big mainframe computers like IBM's are way too expensive—only great big companies are able to buy them. Jobs' and Wozniak's Apple II costs only thirteen hundred dollars. They're selling faster than they can make 'em."

"Hold your horses, Woodrow. I have my own business, right? I've looked into these extravagant IBM computers and all they can do is piddle around with payroll. For the life of me, I can't understand what good *any* computer can do. You expect me to toss money at a crazy idea a bunch of high school children came up with? The answer is no. You hear me? No!"

With misted eyes, Woody crept from the room and drove his ancient Ford back to campus. *That leaves Bill. I hope he made out.*

He parked and attempted to muster the courage to ask Bill if he had better luck. Finally, he walked to the dorm and knocked on his door. The door squeaked open revealing a despondent face.

Without asking, Woody knew. The Apple project was dead.

* * *

Woody decided to escape from the calamity at school and go home for the weekend where he slept and watched TV. Early Monday morning, he approached Martha who wasn't fooled by yet another claim he had a bad headache. "Get dressed before your father finds out you're moping around again."

"I just can't go back to school today. I'm too bummed out."

Martha grimaced. "I don't know why you're down, but you'd better get in gear or your father will cut off your allowance again. Is that what you're after?"

Grumbling, Woody went to his room and dressed. Breakfast had no taste even though Martha had served his favorite—ham and cheese omelet. Outside the kitchenette window, the springtime sun sparkled and a gentle breeze stirred the budding leaves of the oak tree. He didn't notice.

In a complete daze, Woody managed somehow to drive to school. Looking cross, his eight o'clock English teacher asked, "Woody, you with us?" In History, he raised his hand and asked permission to go to the restroom. He didn't return.

At lunch, he found Bill, Jose, and Peggy sitting at the lunch tables, all with glum faces.

"I knew it was a long shot," Jose complained. "We got too busy thinking about code to consider the business end." He propped his chin on his fist. "If that's not bad enough, my grades are not all that good. We kept skipping over too many homework assignments."

The comment jolted Woody. Not only did he push aside homework, but even when he tried, his mind wandered elsewhere. Now, with his head scrambled by the Apple demise, he saw big grade trouble ahead. Summer and graduation were coming up in a month and his father had already been talking to Yale University to find a way to get him enrolled.

All Woody could do was shake his head hoping his grades passed muster.

Bill pulled a pencil from his pocket protector and twirled it. "You know, we didn't have a customer in mind. What if that's the problem? Okay, so we have a matrix, but for what?"

"That's right," Peggy said. "Jose and I do math; Woody and Bill do computers, but who does business?"

Woody stirred.

Bill went on. "Before we call it quits, let's try to nail this down. What kind of business could use our chart? We need to find a business that works with lots of numbers."

Jose and Peggy bobbed their heads.

"Football teams. They have lots of plays?"

"Nah, all they do is memorize a few plays and do them over and over."

Woody brooded.

"High schools?"

"I don't know; they might have a few hundred students each with a few classes, but not much else."

Woody rubbed his chin.

"Movie theaters or the ice rink?"

Heads shook.

"I got it."

Their heads turned toward Woody who was rubbing his fluttering eye.

"Grocery stores. They handle gobs of stuff and have jillions of transactions. Cash registers dinging all the time. I'm thinkin' they are serious number crunchers."

"That kinda makes sense," Bill said.

Jumping to his feet, Woody whooped, "We can save this! I bet every grocery store can afford an Apple and every store has huge inventory that changes every time a shopping cart goes out the door. They have to keep track of stuff that gets too old to sell. They have sales, so prices change. Number crunching up the gazoo!"

Ever the skeptic, Jose asked, "Assuming you're right, how do we show them our program? It's not aimed at them yet. What do we know about their business?"

"It's simple," Woody assured him. "I'll buzz over to Samuel's Grocery after class tomorrow and talk with the manager. They're a nationwide chain, so the possibilities are mind-boggling! I'll explain how we could tailor our chart to match what they do."

"I'll bet the manager of the local store can't make that kind of decision, though," Bill cautioned.

"Fear not, my friend," Woody said. "I'll dazzle them. Our matrix is a wonder! Samuel's is sure to see that. I'll have them in the palm of my hand."

The school bell rang, sending them off to their respective classes. As Peggy and Jose strolled away, Peggy leaned over and whispered, "Sometimes I think Woody needs to take a chill pill. Samuel's? Really?"

"He's got a wild imagination for sure," Jose said. "It's one thing to advertise in the school paper, but another to tackle a nationwide corporation. Time will tell."

* * *

Early the next morning Woody got on the phone and grilled his grudging father about things he had little knowledge of: accounting, inventory, and cash flow. Then, he skipped lunch period and drove to Samuel's

Grocery store. Clutching a folder with a printout of the matrix, he marched confidently into the store. He interrupted a customer at checkout and asked the cashier, "Where's the manager?"

Without pausing, the clerk rang up a bunch of broccoli and tipped his head toward a kiosk against the wall. "The guy in the white shirt."

"Thanks." Eagerly, Woody walked over to the manager.

Eyeing the man's name badge, Woody said, "Mister Hopkins, my name is Woody Lawrence and I'd like to talk with you about a scientific breakthrough."

Hopkins didn't look up and continued thumbing through a stack of cash register receipts.

Woody laid his folder on the counter and tapped his foot. "Mister Hopkins?"

"One moment, young man." The receipts rustled.

Woody tried to tamp down his excitement. Finally, Hopkins looked up and said, "Now, what can I do for you?"

"Okay, what I have here is an accounting and inventory tracking wonder. You'll be amazed." Woody whipped out the diagram and placed it on the counter reverently. "This is a table my friends and I worked up for the new Apple II computer. What it does…"

The phone rang, stopping him mid-sentence. Hopkins snatched it from its cradle, listened a moment, and then blurted, "The supplier promised the canned corn by this morning. Call them right away and tell them…"

Irked, Woody shoved both hands in his pockets and fiddled with loose change.

"No, no. The order was for six cases, not four. You on it? Good." Hopkins hung up the telephone, turned, and said, "Apples? They're in produce over to your left."

"What? Hold on. Apple is a company. They make really great computers." Woody poked his finger at the diagram. "This chart shows how Samuel's could crunch lots of numbers super-fast. Like your inventory. If you look here…"

A harried stock boy rushed up to the counter. "Hoppy, there's some kind of ruckus over by the bakery section," he said breathlessly. "You ought to look into it."

"Violent? Fists?"

"Naw, nothing like that—pissed off customer is all."

"Well, have Susan take care of it—she's the department head. I'm swamped by all this paperwork." Hopkins sighed and turned back to Woody. "Now, what were we talking about?"

"Computers."

"Oh, those. We don't have any in our store. Corporate does, I guess. Not here."

"What I'm saying is…"

The next thirty minutes were filled with chaos, people running around, the phone ringing like a trumpet in a marching band, Hopkins frantically fielding questions. Finally, the manager sputtered, "Look, young man, I don't have time for this. Computers are in the future—maybe ten, twenty years away. Besides, these decisions are made in headquarters, not here. So, if you'll excuse me." He dashed off to some other unknown calamity.

Crushed, Woody silently tucked the diagram back in the folder and went to his car. *I'm not goin' back to school. This time I* ***really*** *have a headache.*

Almost too depressed to get out of bed the next morning, he skipped his usual shower and dressed. Arriving on campus ten minutes before classes began, he found Bill talking with Jose and Peggy in the quad. He clenched his jaw and struggled over, anguish casting a ghoulish look on his face.

"Looks like Samuel's didn't jump in," Bill said with a disappointed look.

All Woody could do was shrug.

"I guess that's all she wrote," Peggy said.

As the others trudged toward their classes, Woody stood alone staring at his shoes.

With only three weeks remaining until summer vacation, Woody tried to improve his grades, but the catastrophe of the Apple project stymied him. He hardly spoke to anyone and when Bill attempted to console him, Woody clammed up, holding misery close to his chest. Finding Woody too weird, Jose and

Peggy gave up all attempts at friendship and went their own way.

The days passed in a dark blur.

On the last day of school, Woody took his report card, hands trembling. Mostly B's and one C. *Coulda been worse.*

Predictably, his father wasn't pleased. Yale University had extremely high standards for entering freshmen. B's simply didn't hack it. "There's a good chance you have thrown your future away, Woodrow!" he yelled into the phone. "You kept fooling around with that silly computer thing and now I'm going to have to pull some serious strings to get you admitted. Good thing I'm a Yale alum."

That weekend Woody could barely get going. He had absolutely no interest in Yale; just wanted to crawl into a hole and die. He'd given up on his mother's return and his passion for science had decayed like old road kill. Adam, his roommate, found Woody still in bed Saturday morning at eleven. "What's happening, man? You should have joined me on the tennis courts. Glorious day." He mopped sweat from his face and stared at the lump underneath the covers. "You sick or something?"

"Go away."

Adam jiggled Woody's bed with his foot. "Come on dude; a bunch of guys are having lunch down at the cafeteria. It'll be a riot—get you out of the dumps."

"Leave me alone!" Woody yelled.

Adam threw up his hands and showered.

While Woody's friends, those who were left, reveled in the summer sunshine, his father issued an edict. "Time you did something productive," he'd said. "You're going to work all summer in my client's factory. All those metal parts they make for the military come out of the lathes and mills with sharp edges. You'll help de-burr them. You know—file the corners, knock off the burrs with a hand grinder. That's something a B minus student should be able to manage."

Even the fantastic glide tests of the Space Shuttle Enterprise failed to draw Woody out of his depression. His future dwelt in the land of metal files and Yale University. His life became garbage.

The Herald American
Monday, September 15, 1980

Heat Wave Cripples South

Hundreds Hospitalized

The blazing summer passed, filled with mind-numbing boredom and cut fingers from his de-burring job.

After several attempts to be friends, his fellow workers gave up and labeled Woody "fucked up beyond recognition." His supervisor tolerated Woody's sloppy work only because he was Woodrow Lawrence the Third, son of the corporate lawyer.

But the big disaster exploded in mid-September: his father called a few markers and got Woody accepted into Yale University.

His freshman year became a complete catastrophe with no friends and no interests. He was assigned to a "Residential College" complete with a roommate he'd be saddled with for the next four years. A comparative literature major, the mousey guy was a fool lost in the dense clouds of Chaucer and Shakespeare and Woody discarded any hope of becoming friends. Acutely despondent about the Apple debacle, Woody barely managed C's in the hated pre-law classes. Thankfully the grades were good enough to avoid probation, so his father never knew he'd been teetering on the brink.

The year slogged by in a depressing fog.

That summer, he returned to the burr-bench and fingers covered by Band-Aids. Woody became an empty shell devoid of aspiration or sense of worth.

The crisp days of fall found Woody back at Yale, now a sophomore. Morose, he sulked from class to class. One afternoon out of sheer boredom, he sat on a shady bench alongside a footpath and gnawed on a hot dog he bought from a cart vendor. "This thing tastes like poodle puckey," he groused. From time to time, students would stroll by chatting. He became irritated if one glanced at him, but a hippy-looking guy sitting on the other side of the path annoyed him even more. He had one of those new Walkman things and hummed loudly along with some discordant tune that leaked out around his headphones. His head bobbed and his fingers rapped out a beat on a folder beside him on the bench. Provoked to his limit, Woody gathered up his books, preparing to leave.

"Excuse me? May I sit here?"

Woody looked up and saw a striking young girl dressed in Kelly green jeans and a trim-fitting sweater. A wide leather belt cinched in her narrow waist and a bright smile graced her face. Woody forgot the jerk with the Walkman and pulled his books to him, making room on the bench. "Sure."

She eased onto the bench, crossed her legs and set a bundle of sheet music on her lap. "Thanks. It's a long way from the damn music hall to my dorm. Thought I'd rest a moment."

Addled, Woody juggled strange thoughts and emotions. Speechless, he simply stared at the girl while his right eye went into a nearly forgotten dance.

"You always so talkative?"

"What? Oh, yes—no." Struggling not to look like a dolt, he pointed at the sheet music. "Like music?"

"Like it? Hell yes—it's my life; it's my major." She glanced at the fellow across the way with the

Walkman and pointed. "See? Music is everywhere. They keep saying that science is the big thing, but I'm going to make sure that music takes over the world."

"Takes over?"

"Well, not really, but you know what I'm saying."

Woody nodded.

"Say, I'm Angela Andros. I go by Angie. You?" She stuck out her hand.

Delicately, like he was about to touch a piece of heaven, he took her hand. "Woody."

"Last name?"

"Lawrence. Woody Lawrence."

"What are you majoring in, Woody Lawrence?" she asked, a smile lighting up her face.

"I, well, I guess it's gonna be law after I graduate with a Bachelor's." He scowled as he spoke.

Angie's peal of laughter startled him. "You guess? What kind of crappy major is that?"

"Well, you know," Woody said, drawing in a deep breath. "My father insists I become an attorney like him."

She tapped his arm, a girlish wrist-motion tap. "You sound soooo enthused."

Jolted by her touch, bewilderment swept over Woody's mind and he battled to align his thoughts. Abruptly, he blurted, "I hate law!"

Eyes wide as a child in a Keane painting, Angie leaned back and said, "Damn, I guess you *do* hate law. Now I have to ask what you *do* like. What's your passion?" She tugged at the bottom of her bright-colored sweater, straightening it.

Woody suspected that he didn't have any kind of passion. Not since Samuel's. And why should he have this conversation with a complete stranger? He'd come to cherish his misery; was that his passion? He glanced sideways at Angie's expectant grin and knew he couldn't tell her that. *She seems somehow interested in me?* He flipped through the mental file of past events: the first moon landing, matchstick rockets, the launch of Apollo 17, the Space Shuttle, Apple computer…

Haltingly, Woody said, "I have a thing for rockets and computers; they turn me on. My father took me to see the launch of Apollo 17 and told me he was doing me a big favor, but he lied. He had business in Florida and let me tag along. He's making me take pre-law stuff so I can follow in his footsteps. But I'm crazy about rockets and space." He went on to tell her about the huge rocket blasting off and how it deeply moved him, realizing he *did* have a passion.

He crossed his arms tightly across his chest, ashamed to reveal family problems and wild tales about rockets to this striking apparition sitting next to him. "I don't know why I'm telling you all this. It's kinda embarrassing, you know."

Angie pursed her lips. *This guy is somewhere between a basket case and an inspiration* She reached over and patted Woody's shoulder. "So, you like science stuff and I'm into music. Does that mean we can't be friends? You know; opposites attract, right? You could tell me more about space and I could talk about Beethoven."

Woody lightly rubbed his shoulder where Angie had touched him. "You wanna be friends?"

* * *

The folded piece of paper in Woody's hand felt like it could burn clean through his palm. Gently, he opened it up and reread the numbers he'd already memorized—Angie's phone number. He reached for the telephone and then reconsidered. *No way. I've no use for music, she doesn't do science. This is goin' nowhere.* For fifteen minutes he stewed, staring at the phone while recalling the catastrophe his mother's desertion had cast upon him. The full dilemma suddenly became clear to him: he'd had no experience with girls. None. Although his acne had pretty much cleared up and his glasses no longer bothered him, he found refuge in science more comforting than venturing into the scary world of female companionship. He'd gotten along okay with Peggy at LeMay, but her rejection over the Apple fiasco affirmed his "solution" to the girl problem. But Angie was different—a smile to die for, contagious laughter, and zeal for life. Plus, she'd given him her phone number.

He pushed aside his textbook on political science, picked up the phone, and dialed. "Hi, Angie, it's Woody."

"Woody! Glad you called. I've been wondering where you've been. It's been three days, you know."

The sound of her bubbly voice made him quiver. In the background he heard some kind of music playing, a symphony or whatever. He tried to form a few words, but couldn't.

"Woody?"

"Uh, yeah. Hi. Thought I'd call to see how you're doin'."

"I'm doing great, now that you've phoned. What's going on?"

"Nothin' much. Trying to study."

A tinkling giggle leapt from the receiver. "You're studying to get into Yale Law? You hate the damn law. Maybe you should study music? Like Mozart's Fortieth Symphony I'm listening to right now."

Ignoring the question, Woody blurted, "Want to have a burger with me?"

A stunned silence. "Hell yes! None of that McDonald's stuff though. Meet me at Lillie's Cafe?"

"What? You want to get together right now?"

"You'd rather study law?" Angie quipped.

"See you in fifteen."

* * *

Nervous, Woody walked into Lillie's, a typical run-of-the-mill college town eatery. Large posters of Handsome Dan, Yale's bulldog mascot, adorned the walls. Having never been in the place, his eyes jerked from counter to booth to a small waiting area, searching for Angie. She wasn't to be seen. *She's changed her mind and isn't coming*. Panting from racing to the restaurant, he looked at his watch. *Well, maybe I'm early.*

A young hostess showed him to a booth. "Just you?"

"No. I'm expecting another." *I hope.*

Woody's eyes snapped back and forth from his watch to front door to watch, his glance constantly shifting. All the while, he fiddled with the silverware, making a soft ringing sound. Seconds passed, then minutes.

The front door swung open and there she was, framed by sunlight. Like a silly kid at a circus, Woody jumped up and waved. "Hi! Over here!"

"Sorry I'm a little late. I had to change clothes."

"No problem."

She looked gorgeous. Not in the Farrah Fawcett or Lynda Carter sort of way, but in an Angie way. Her spontaneous smile, glittering blue eyes, and soft hair fluttering around her face, put Hollywood glamour to shame. She'd donned a calf-length patterned skirt and lacy top that made Woody's duds look grungy. A little embarrassed, he groped for words. "You're lookin' nice."

She waved a dismissive hand. "Now that we're friends, what would you like to talk about? How about the counterpoint in Beethoven's Ninth Symphony?" Her wide grin betrayed her playfulness.

"No, I was thinking more about the hypergolic reaction in rocket motor propellants," Woody parried.

"Too bland. How about some law? Maybe Roe vs. Wade?"

"Black hole event horizons?"

Their laughter reverberated through the restaurant, making some patrons give them an annoyed look.

Woody didn't notice the tension in his shoulders had vanished and that the pervasive sense of doom he'd carried for months had evaporated. Surprisingly, after a heavy dose of salt, the burger and fries tasted great. Easy banter, liberally laced with raucous laughter zipped across the table. Woody's world had abruptly changed.

After two and a half hours and four Coke refills, nasty stares from the restaurant owner suggested they might pay the bill and leave. After Woody had tugged his wallet from his pocket and paid the tab, they walked out chatting and giggling. "Walk you to your dorm?" suggested Woody.

"Aren't you the gentleman?" With a sly expression, she added, "But you can't come in."

Woody's face turned bright red. "No, I wasn't thinking...I mean... of course not."

Happy in the late afternoon sunlight, they strolled to her dorm. There, Angie playfully pecked Woody on the cheek. "Let's do this again, okay? Maybe tomorrow?"

Stunned by the kiss, Woody gasped and gathered his wits. "Yeah. Sure." Suddenly, a mischievous grin spread across his face. "I know what, there's a lecture about acid-base titration in the chemistry lab at ten tomorrow. Should be fun."

Angie poked him with one of her girly-wristy gestures and said, "Call me."

* * *

That very night he did. "Hey. How about a movie tomorrow night?"

"Tomorrow? No, I can't; I have to study for a quiz on Vivaldi. He wrote hundreds of pieces—boggles my mind. This is the first test of the year and I have no idea what the professor will ask."

In the background, Woody heard music that sounded like someone sawing on a piece of sheet metal. Screech, screech. Disappointment settled in his stomach like an anvil. "You sure? Some good films are playing."

"What about Friday night?"

"That's two days away! Help me out here."

"Sorry."

For Woody, the next forty-eight hours slogged by like a hibernating sloth. They'd met briefly between classes and decided that Friday's dinner was going to be theater popcorn at the movies. Woody volunteered to check out times the various features started. So, on Friday afternoon he called.

"Hi, Angie; I found a super flick that starts at 7:15 tonight."

"What is it?"

"It's called *The Shining*. From a Steven King novel."

"Yuck! That's a gross horror thing. I detest stupid horror films. I've been looking at the paper and *The Coal Miner's Daughter* got rave reviews. Lots of music, you know."

Woody's jaw clenched tight. *Not a musical; I can't deal with a syrupy bunch of singing*. "Well, if that's what you want. I'm not really big on musicals, though."

"Oh, it's not one of those big productions where the actors break into crappy songs about silly things nobody cares about. It's a true story about Loretta Lynn. You know, country music."

He'd never heard of Loretta Lynn and what little country music he'd been exposed to had nauseated him. Woody took stock of his situation. *The movie doesn't matter – Angie does. This is only our second date and the time to make a good impression is now. Indulge her.* "Loretta whoever sounds fine. What time does it start?"

"7:25 at the Meralta."

"Great. I'll pick you up at seven."

Woody spent the next hour going over his old Ford with a damp rag making sure not to leave streaks. He cleaned the windows and dusted the inside, taking extra care with the passenger seat. A shower, a swish of mouthwash, and fresh clothes completed his preparations. Nearly an hour remained until the big moment, so Woody trimmed his fingernails and fidgeted.

When he drove up, Angie was sitting on a bench under a streetlight waiting for him. Woody dashed around the car, opened the door and waved her inside with a dramatic sweep of his arm. "Madam," he said with his best imitation of a British butler.

Too nervous to say much, he drank in Angie's ongoing chitchat while driving.

"I aced the exam about Vivaldi," she said. "Teach went easy on us, asked about Vivaldi's most popular pieces: the *Four Seasons* and *Concerti con Molti Strumenti*. This class is going to be easy!"

"Oh sure…Vivaldi."

Angie giggled. "How are your law classes?"

"I'm not taking real law classes. It's pre-law. I'm doin' American History and a computer course my father doesn't know about. Poly Sci too. That sort of stuff."

"Didn't you say you're a computer guru?"

Woody shrugged. "This is different from what I was doing."

The long line in front of the box-office crept as Woody fidgeted awkwardly alongside Angie.

"See, *Coal Miner's Daughter* is really popular," Angie said. "You're going to love it."

"I'm sure I will," Woody replied. *A bunch of hillbilly singing. No way.*

Once inside, they hustled over to the snack bar and picked up a big bag of popcorn, two Cokes, a box of Good and Plenty, and another of Nerds. Thus fortified, they settled into their seats.

Sure enough, the music, particularly "Blue Moon of Kentucky," twanged and thumped on Woody's ears. They did a weird foot stomping dance that caught his eye. "What's that?" he whispered to Angie.

"It's called clogging."

"Hmmm."

Disgusted, he squirmed while a bunch of hicks fooled around on the screen. Woody wanted to reach over and take Angie's hand, but lacked the courage. Then a scene in a bar came on where Loretta looked shy and uneasy before singing her first ever song in front of a crowd.

"There He Goes," she warbled. At first, the crowd just drank and talked loudly, but Loretta kept singing. The tune caught Woody's attention and he found himself lightly tapping his foot. He noticed Angie patted her hand on the arm of the chair in time to the music. Slowly, the crowd noise in the movie softened and Loretta's confidence grew until her voice swelled and captured the audience.

Wow, Woody thought. A sideways glance revealed Angie's hand, rapping out the rhythm.

Inspired by the singer's boldness, he slyly took Angie's hand and was rewarded by a smile and a squeeze.

Woody saw little of the remaining movie, his heart pounding and breathing irregularly. After the film ended and everyone jostled out, Woody gingerly took her hand once more. "I can't believe Loretta and that Dew person got married when she was only thirteen. Is that true?"

"I think it is. She married Doolittle; his nickname was spelled D…o…o, not D…e…w."

"Can't hear the difference."

On the way back to Angie's dorm, Woody kept humming "There He Goes."

Hearing him, Angie said, "I guess you liked the movie, huh?"

"Sure did." He found himself surprised that he actually enjoyed it. Parts of it anyway.

He pulled to a stop in front of Angie's place and switched off the ignition. "I had a won…"

Angie took his face in her hands and kissed him soundly. Startled, Woody didn't know what to do with his hands. Finally, he caught her up in his arms and the kiss moved from warm to passionate to fiery. His fingers found her hair, soft, silky, glowing blond in the glow of a distant streetlight. Woody's world became Angie; his car, the dorm, Yale University all faded into nothingness. "Oh my God," he moaned.

Angie disentangled herself and pushed him away. "I'm thinking this is enough for tonight, don't you think?"

Panting, he said, "No! I mean sure if you want to quit."

An impish grim spread across her face. "Just for now. Call me tomorrow." With that, she jumped from the car and sprinted into her dorm.

* * *

Angie's phone rang and rang until the answering machine picked up. "I can't come to the phone right now, so..."

Disgusted, Woody hung up. His mind flashed back to the previous night. What did she mean "Just for now?" His imagination flitted from kisses to mysterious wonders of Angie's body—her trim waist, her pert breasts.

His life had become completely foreign to him. Where had the rockets and computers gone? Apple II no longer appeared in his thinking. Grocery stores? Bill Butler and Peggy—gone. All had become Angie and kisses. All had become anticipation of more passionate kisses. Woody couldn't recognize himself.

That afternoon, he finally reached her. "Where have you been? Been calling all day…"

"At class, silly. Haven't you?"

Woody gulped. "No. I've been trying all day to get a hold of you."

"Dammit, you should really try to get to class from time to time, Woody." Laughter leapt from the phone. "By the way, I've been thinking about last night."

"Me too!"

"You want to get together again tonight? I've decided to show you something special."

Fireworks went off in Woody's head. *Special? What kind of special?* He wondered how Angie would look naked. "Special? Yeah, I'm ready!" *But maybe her idea of special is a concert or opera.* His chest tightened.

"Pick me up around eight, okay?"

"Sure. Where are we going?"

"Surprise." A giggle trickled from the phone before the click.

Woody stared at the handset for a long time before setting it in its cradle. His watch told him that eight o'clock was forever away.

* * *

That night he parked in front of Angie's dorm fifteen minutes early, and not wanting to appear stupid-anxious, decided to wait in the car. Jittery, he managed to hold off for five minutes before going into the lobby and calling Angie from the desk phone.

She bounced down the stairs dressed in embroidered jeans and a knit sweater with images of lambs on it. But it was her bright smile that caught his eye.

They kissed lightly. "You have me on pins and needles," Woody said excitedly. "Where are we going? What's going down?"

Angie took his arm. "You'll see."

Following her directions, Woody drove in the general direction of Long Island Sound. "Gonna hit water pretty soon."

Angie patted his thigh. "Turn here."

Shortly they drew up to a little harbor and stopped in a parking area next to the boat moorings. Puzzled, Woody asked, "Where are we?"

With a chuckle and another of her usual girlie-wristy hand gestures, Angie said, "It's the Pequannock Yacht Club, silly. I wondered if your wealthy father might have a boat here. My daddy does."

"Father is way too busy for a yacht. A 'frivolity' he'd call it." Woody looked out over the harbor. "Where are all the boats? The place is half deserted. Not very popular, I guess."

"A lot of the members take their boats out of the water in the fall because they're not used during wintertime. Daddy doesn't. Says it's too much of a damn hassle for such a big boat as his."

Woody nodded. "Why did you bring me here?"

"Oh, I thought you'd like to see Daddy's yacht. It's pretty fancy. Forty-five feet long."

Curious, Woody shrugged. "Why not?"

They walked up to a big wrought iron gate and Angie deftly unlocked it. "This way." She took his hand and briskly led him along the wooden walkway between the boat slips. "We're at the end of C dock," she explained.

Nearly all the craft were wrapped in white canvas covers, which disappointed Woody because he would have liked to check them out. Nevertheless, Angie's hand felt warm in his.

The harbor was completely devoid of people and the early cold snap nipped at Woody's nose. He heard a distant bell clanging softly and figured the noise came from a buoy rocking on the tide.

"This is it!" cried Angie pointing at yet another canvas tent. "Careful, don't trip on that electrical cable. Daddy heats the boat year around. Claims it stops mildew."

"Does the boat have a name?"

"Sure it does! Guess what it is."

Woody shrugged.

Angie lifted her chin and waggled her head back and forth. "Meet *Angie's Raft*. Isn't that too cool?" Her laughter echoed across the water. She turned and pointed. "Out there is Long Island Sound. Every summer we cruise the Sound for days at a time." She fished in her purse and brought out another key and slipped it into a padlock. "Help me unzip this damn thing."

In a jiffy they clambered inside and Woody was surprised how warm it felt. "Let's do a tour," said Angie. She pointed to the kitchen, calling it the galley. It looked small, but had a sink, stove, granite counters, and polished wood cabinets. "Wow! Very elegant," Woody said.

"Come with me," Angie instructed. "Here's the dining area and up that ladder is the helm where you drive the boat; man the helm in sailor talk." Walking toward the bow, she rapped on a mahogany door. "This is the head—potty to you, and the last is the master bedroom."

Woody was impressed by the wide bed, antique side tables, and the soft lighting.

A leer spread across Angie's face. "I believe we have unfinished business, Mr. Lawrence." She pushed Woody onto the bed. "No crappy car backseats for this girl." She pulled her sweater over her head and unhooked her bra.

Woody's eyes popped from his head.

Thus, began frequent visits to the Pequannock Yacht Club and excursions into the land of ecstasy and passion.

* * *

Woody gasped when he looked at his Political Science test paper. A large "D" had been scrawled in bold red ink at the top of the page. *Dang, too much yacht club, not enough studying.* Dismayed, he trudged to his computer class. He took his seat and tucked the Poly Sci exam into a folder. Dismayed, he wondered what Angie would say when she heard about the "D." He dreaded the possibility that she'd suggest fewer jaunts to daddy's yacht, so he decided not to mention it. He knew his father would be furious and resolved to do better. To head off possible problems, he decided to give him a rare phone call to say how wonderful things were.

* * *

The computer instructor walked to the front of the room and said, "All right people, I've some interesting news for you. We've spent most of our time talking about IBM mainframe computers and punch cards, but not much about Apple. There's a new program out for the Apple II; it's called Visicalc. Actually, it's been around for a few months, but suddenly it's become big news. It's put Apple on the map." He paused and licked his lips. "So, here's the deal. They call it a spreadsheet. It has a table of boxes where numbers and functions like addition and multiplication can be entered. The program is aimed at serious number crunching. To expand..."

Woody leapt to his feet yelling, "That's my program! They stole it! I can prove I had it first!"

Stunned, the entire class stared at him. "Okay, okay, young man. Simmer down," the professor cautioned. "No need to shout."

His face as red as the "D" on his poly sci exam, Woody sputtered. "No. No. Me and Bill. Jose and Peggy. We did it! Took forever working in the physics lab. Used their Apple II. Even Colonel…" He stared right and left at the snickering students and wanted to scream at them. Abruptly, he snatched up his books and papers and bolted to the door. He turned, shot a livid glance at the professor and screamed, "This…is…horseshit!"

That night, he canceled a planned trip to the yacht club, so Angie knew something serious had gone down. In the lounge of Woody's dorm, he sat hunched over in despair while Angie rubbed his shoulders. "I haven't seen you like this since we first met. What's the deal?"

"They stole my matrix."

"Who?"

"Some outfit put out a program called VisiCalc. All our work, ripped off."

"How do you know they swiped your stuff? Is it the same as what you took to the grocery store?"

"Same basic idea as ours. I didn't stick around for the details. Didn't have to."

"If it's true they stole it, how did they get your program? What do you call it? Code?"

"Who knows? Gould? Mockli? Maybe Jose or Peggy. They're the only ones who knew about it. Not that it matters now; VisiCorp is cranking it out like crazy and I'm out of the picture. Look, I don't want to talk about this anymore. I'm going upstairs to bed."

Aimless, Woody drifted through the next two weeks while his grades plummeted. Angie couldn't find a way to raise his spirits and trips to the yacht club ceased. One afternoon, Angie was enjoying a brisk moment in the quad while Woody sat comatose alongside her on a bench, arms crossed, eyes closed.

Being a music-major, Angie had justified the purchase of a new Walkman cassette player and was listening to a pop song. Head bobbing, she frantically scratched notes in her notebook.

"What are you doing? The bench is shaking like a California earthquake," Woody snapped.

Angie lifted the headphones from her ears. "What?"

"I said you're jiggling the bench."

"Chill. I'm listening to a super song. It's an assignment about POP music. Came out last year so it's a little out of date, but it had been at the top of the charts. Has rhythm, you hear?" She held out the headphones to Woody.

He started to push her hand away, but the raucous piano caught his ear. He paused, head tilted. Bits of lyrics penetrated his sour mood.

"'cause I'm all right"

"this is my life"

"victim of circumstance"

"I still belong"

Woody's eyes met Angie's. "What's this song?" he asked.

"It's a tune called 'My Life' by Billy Joel. Cool, huh?"

With a grimace, Woody said, "It sounds like this Billy guy is talking directly to me."

Angie raised her eyebrow. "What do you mean?"

"He told me I'm all right. Of course I'm not, but I wish I were. Victim of circumstance. Hell yes, I am!"

An impish grin swept Angie's face. "He also said 'this is my life', right? What is your life, Woody? Where the hell you going? You plan to stay bummed out for the rest of your life over some silly computer program? We haven't been to the yacht club since forever."

A profound thought crept through his mind, "'cause I'm all right." Woody took a deep breath and laid his hand on Angie's arm. His eye twitching, he said, "Let's go get a Coke."

* * *

Woody couldn't get "My Life" out of his head. The lyrics flew like an arrow aimed directly at his brain, at his depression. He kept pondering the nature of his life. *What's with rockets?* He dredged up memories of fourth grade and the matchstick rockets. How excited he'd been, how the kids roared their approval, how the principal and his father had berated him, grounded him.

His model of the Space Shuttle. The glory of the achievement. The accolades of the other kids. The crushing disaster of The King's scorn and the beating he took to prove to others that King did it.

The Apple II fiasco. Soaring expectations, grinding hour upon hour of experimentation. Victory had been in sight, only to be extinguished by a distracted grocery store manager. Rejection by his friends. Banished to menial summers at the factory by his father.

Then there was the awakening brought on by Angie. She'd opened up a new world for him. Spasms of joy at the Pequannock Yacht Club. The feeling of personal worth she brought to him. All in jeopardy because of the cruelty of VisiCalc and the resulting crushing disappointment.

Heaving a big sigh, he wondered, *why does the pendulum always have to swing? Something in my nature pushes me into wild leaps of imagination. At the same time, it seems that my adventures are doomed to failure. Ah well, better to have loved and lost…* Softly singing Billy Joel's tune, he murmured, "'cause I'm all right." He smacked a fist into his palm. "I wasn't, but now I am."

* * *

Angie's Raft gently rocked as a nearby motorboat eased into its slip. Woody wrapped his arm around Angie and purred, "That was spectacular, my love."

She cuddled up and lightly kissed his cheek. "You're telling me that Billy Joel's song triggered this immense change in your outlook?"

"Weird, isn't it? I've never had any interest in music until now, but that song blew me away. Of course, you being big into music might have something to do with my newfound interest."

With a giggle, Angie poked his rib. "You've touched just the tip of the iceberg, Woody. Wait until I introduce you to Beethoven, Strauss, or Pachelbel. That's serious music!"

"You want me to vomit all over you?"

Boisterous laughter filled the yacht. "You wouldn't dare!" Angie sat up. "How about a glass of that champagne we bought to celebrate your fresh start? It should be cold by now. While you're at it, grab that packet of cheese from the grocery bag we grabbed on the way."

"I'd rather snuggle, but why not?"

Woody popped the cork and they clinked glasses. The bubbles tickled their noses and a contented silence filled the cabin. After a while, Angie said, "Are you ever going to work on computers again? I suspect you're very good at it."

Woody scowled. "After Apple and VisiCalc kicked me in the balls? Right now, computers are my enemy. Why do you ask?"

"Ever hear of a synthesizer? You know, electronic music? All the kids are talking about them and I thought you might want to look into it."

"Yeah, I've heard snatches of it here and there. They sound like a cat going through a wringer."

"You're being stubborn," Angie laughed. "Seriously, some of it is damn good. I'll have to play a song or two for you sometime. The trouble is they have a very distinctive sound; the heavy metal and hard rock bands go for it a lot. Still, there are a few nice pieces out there."

"Where are you going with this?"

With a twinkle in her eye, Angie said, "Synthesizers are nothing but electric pianos. They often toss in a few electronic gimmicks, but nothing of consequence. So, I was wondering what could be done if a synthesizer was computerized. Take your matrix thing for example. What would happen if you plugged musical notes into those little boxes you told me about? Huh?" She held up her champagne glass and sipped, a mischievous grin on her lips.

Woody waved his hand. "That's crazy. Why would anyone…" Suddenly, his brows drew together in a serious expression. "You know…" He rubbed his chin and squinted. "In the matrix, we plugged in numbers. Sound is nothing but frequencies—numbers. I suppose I could make the matrix make sounds, even notes, but what's the point?"

Angie finished off her champagne. "Do you think a computer could change a cat's screech into a mellow purr? Turn harsh synthesizer racket into a delicate oboe note?"

"What's an oboe?" Woody broke out into roaring laughter. "Dear Angie, all of a sudden you've got me thinking."

* * *

And think he did—at length. The first thing, he checked out what an oboe looked like and gasped in disbelief. *It's just a tiny stick of wood. Kinda like a clarinet with a thyroid problem. I bet it sounds like an old man's wheeze.* He pulled out a printout of the matrix and studied it, mentally putting frequencies in the blocks. He went to the local music store and bought a record featuring synthesizer music, which only reinforced his disgust. Within a day, Woody discovered his ignorance of music had become an insurmountable roadblock. The answer, of course, could be found with Angie.

She was astonished when he asked, "I'm in big trouble, Angie. What's an octave?"

"Let's go over all that tomorrow. It's a Saturday so we'll have time. Right now, I'm exhausted from schoolwork. Instead, let's grab a burger on the way to *Angie's Raft*, okay?"

The corners of Woody's mouth drooped. "Well, yeah; we could, I guess, but I'm really stuck. Ideas are bouncing around in my head—good ones I hope." He frowned. "How about you spend tonight teaching me music?"

Thunderstruck, Angie gasped. "Are you serious? Is our honeymoon over already?"

"It's your fault, you know; suggesting I could combine a computer with a synthesizer to make music. I've always had this problem, getting a crazy idea and working it to death without letup. I'm hooked!"

Skeptical, Angie scowled. "Tell me this. Is your zeal about computers or about music? I remember you saying that you had no interest in music. None. So why should I waste time explaining what a damn octave is?"

Woody pressed his lips together. "You're right. I said that. But then you had me listen to Billy Joel. The guy has something. Sure, it was the lyrics that blew me away, but the tune keeps hanging around in my head. I hum it all the time. So, I'd have to say my enthusiasm is for both music and computers."

"You realize you're nuts, right? And I'm nuts to be nuts about you. Let's go over to the cafe and have that burger and I'll explain what an octave is."

They became regular customers at the restaurant. Woody struggled mightily with the foreign language of music while Angie picked up tidbits of computer lingo. Late night hours would find them head-to-head in serious conversation over tepid cups of coffee.

Almost immediately, a big problem arose. No computer. Afraid to approach his father, Woody pooled his leftover allowance money with Angie's meager stash and made a down payment on an Apple II. In that way, the yacht club took on an additional role: a scientific laboratory as well as love nest. As *Angie's Raft* languished in the winter gloom, they abruptly abandoned Lillie's Cafe.

"It's really simple, Woody. Look at this sheet music. The staff is sort of like your matrix. Think of a graph of five lines and four spaces. These spots on the staff represent different notes, different frequencies."

"Yeah, but your 'spots' are all different. Some are hollow; some have tails. It's all mixed up."

Angie chuckled. "The hollow ones are called whole notes; they're held for a long time. If it has a flag, it's an eighth note. See this one here," said Angie pointing, "it's solid with two flags. That's a sixteenth note having a very short duration tone."

"Araggh!" hollered Woody. "You might as well be talking Chinese or something!"

"Be patient, my love." She rubbed the back of his neck. "Let's start over, okay?"

Water softly lapped against the hull and cries of seagulls punctuated their solemn conversation. An hour passed. Then two. Woody threw up his hands in exasperation. "Time out! My mind has turned into Jell-O. Help me understand why I like 'My Life'. The words really talked to me. Got me thinking. But the tune is cool. I don't understand why."

"You tell me. What's the first thing you heard?"

"Drums, I guess."

"Just drums, or the rhythm?"

"Same thing, right?" Angie's glare told him he'd erred. "Well, the piano really rocked too," he muttered defensively.

"Did you hear the guitars, clarinet, and back-up singers too?"

"What? I guess I didn't sort all that out."

With a groan, Angie grabbed her Walkman, shoved in a cassette, and pushed the play button. She held one earphone to Woody's ear and the other to hers. "Listen."

Woody's hand patted the arm of the chair in time to the music. "There," murmured Angie. "The guitars."

Woody grunted and smiled.

The piano rattled rapidly while Joel sang. "There. Hear the clarinet?" Angie asked.

"Oh, yeah!"

Soon, the song ended, leaving Woody grinning.

"Did you notice that when the back-up singers came in, they weren't singing the same notes as Joel?"

"They weren't?"

Angie shook her head in dismay. "I'll play it again. Listen this time."

"I have a better idea," Woody smirked. "Let's finish off that bottle of wine and then do a little whoopee, okay?"

With a laugh, Angie scolded, "All men are alike. Their brains are in their damn crotch."

The Herald American

Tuesday, December 4, 1980

John Lennon Murdered!

Killer Apprehended in Manhattan

Woody and Angie stared at the newspaper with glazed eyes. "Why would anyone want to shoot him?" Angie murmured. "His last album with Yoko was inspiring. 'Double Fantasy,' it's called. About being in love."

"Sometimes I think the world has gone crazy," Woody said. "All Lennon wanted was peace and love."

"Tell you what, let's go over to that music store; A—Sharp it's called, and buy the album, Okay? Kinda like a memorial."

* * *

The weeks flew by and Woody was inundated with major and minor keys, octaves, harmonies. Sharps and flats, time signatures. Whenever Angie overwhelmed him, Woody retreated to his new computer, fiddling around making musical notes on it. As winter faded, the encroaching springtime presented special problems. Angie's parents began taking the boat out on weekends. That meant the Apple had to be shuttled back and forth to the dorm. Wine glasses had to be washed and put away. Sheets laundered, refrigerator emptied, candy wrappers and sacks of groceries disposed of. The weekends found them at Lillie's once more. Both struggled to find time to keep their grades up. In spite of the daily whirl, Woody, inspired by Angie, began making real musical progress.

One Saturday at lunch, Woody announced, "Angie, I've been thinking all along and now I've decided for sure. I'm going to follow up on your suggestion to hook up the Apple to a synthesizer to see what I can come up with. What do you know about synthesizers?"

"Not much more than I know about computers." A wide grin blossomed across her face. "They have two or three synths in the music department. I'm thinking I could check one out if I can prove I'm working on something for one of my classes."

"Here's what you tell 'em. Say you're going to hook up a computer to the synthesizer and come up with a whole new kind of music. Tell 'em you'll put on a concert with the new compositions."

"Isn't that a little premature? Sure, you're coming along, but we've never hooked up your new Apple to a synth. You sticking your neck out?"

"Naw. I've done this sort of thing all my life. Nothing ventured, nothing gained, they say."

This man is wild! His thinking knows no bounds and I love him for it. With a chuckle, she said, "I'll look into getting us a synth."

* * *

"I had to promise the goddamn moon, but I can borrow a synthesizer from the music department," Angie said, arms thrown wide. "I'll pick it up this afternoon."

The setting sun touched the top of the buildings as Angie staggered from the music room.

"Help me, Woody. This thing's a little on the heavy side."

"No problem. Let me have it." Deftly, he set it in the trunk of his car. He folded back the flaps of the carton and peeked inside. "Look at that! There are as many knobs on this thing as the control panel for an Apollo moon launch!" Running to the driver's door, he called out, "Hop in; I can't wait to fiddle with this wonder." Full of excitement, Woody raced toward the yacht.

"Slow down, you're gonna get a ticket!" Angie yelled.

Woody just grinned and sped through a yellow light. Lurching to a halt at the yacht club, he hoisted the synthesizer from the trunk. "Can you bring the Apple, Angie?" Panting as he trudged along the walkway to the boat, he said, "This is going to be a pain. Lugging the computer back and forth is bad enough, but now we'll have the synth too."

"Well, we can't leave them here on the yacht now that my parents are taking it out occasionally."

"I know. I know." He eased down the ladder into the boat and set the carton on the table next to the galley. Gingerly, he opened the cardboard flaps and pulled out the synth. "Wow, look at this." He caressed the black cabinet in wonder.

"It's called a Korg MS-20," Angie said. "I brought the instruction booklet too. Sorry to say, I don't know a thing about it. It has a short piano keyboard, so maybe I can play something on it."

Woody slid the Apple alongside. "I don't know where to start. Guess I might take a look at the instructions." Turning pages, he muttered, "Monophonic lead, bass synth, patch-cords, analog oscillators…" He frowned in confusion. "This is going to be tough to get my head around. Good thing I'm into science."

Angie grinned. "Plug it in, you nut. Isn't that always the first step? Even a music major knows that."

And the days passed. Woody patched the Apple into the Korg and experimented. High pass, low pass, band reject. A tune that brought laughter to Angie's lips. Bypassing the filters to make crunch and screech noises. Programming the Apple to make symphonic sound—all often diverted by forays into the bedroom.

When Angie's parents decided to take a three-week vacation to Europe, Angie and Woody decided to set up housekeeping on the yacht. Reluctantly, Woody tried to keep up with school, but Angie's music tutoring sessions and the Korg often took precedence. By mid-April, Woody had worked up three special songs unlike current pop or synthesizer music. "Angie, you have to listen to these—they're *exactly* what I've been looking for." He fired up the Apple and Korg and sprawled on a chair, eyes glittering.

She listened carefully, the way a music critic would. "Woody, it's curious how these songs combine symphonic sounds with the rhythms of Caribbean music. The melodies are interesting." *These are REALLY different,* she thought. *He's created some curious phrasing, and a weird structure. In reality, I'm not sure if it will go.*

Beaming, Woody proclaimed, "It's time for my debut. You've said the music department would let us use the little courtyard just outside the auditorium. Tell them we're ready. I'll make up some posters to hang around campus. Something like 'Dazzle your ears with a brand-new kind of song.' We'll be famous!"

His mind flipped back to his fading memory of his mother. *She'd be proud. I miss her. Even the Christmas cards have stopped coming.*

Laughing, Angie threw her arms around Woody's neck and kissed him. "You're nuts, but I think you're right. I believe your enthusiasm could move mountains." *I hope the music will too.*

Woody took Angie's hand and led her to the bedroom.

* * *

The next morning Angie solidified arrangements to use the grassy courtyard. The audience would sit on the ground or stand because chairs wouldn't be provided. After listening to Angie's explanation about Woody's blending of computers and synthesizers, the department chair vowed to attend the premier of "a revolution in music."

Woody dashed to the school's bookstore and bought poster board and colored markers. The next morning found him pasting his signs in prominent locations. Exuberance churned in his gut and visions of accolades spun wildly in his mind. *They're gonna be amazed.*

Two days later on a sunny spring afternoon, Woody set up his rig on a table in the courtyard. Angie had arranged for the music department to lend them an amplifier and speakers, so they strung extension cords and wire, giggling as they went.

"That's it," said Woody. "It's an hour before we begin, so let's sit in the shade and rehearse our spiel."

After a while, a few students wandered into the area and were warmly welcomed by Woody and Angie. Soon, the crowd grew to perhaps a hundred and Woody swaggered about, holding court. At last, he strode to the table and announced, "Okay everyone, you are about to hear what happens when a synthesizer mates with a computer. It's like music and science making love."

He was rewarded with scattered laughter.

"Music has been in a rut since the times of Gregorian Chants. Bach, Beethoven, and their imitators will put you to sleep. In the thirties, big bands all sounded alike—boring. Rock and roll put saxophones on the map, but little else. This afternoon will be different. Men have walked on the moon and a few bucks will buy you a ticket on the Concorde airliner, a 1,300 miles per hour kick in the pants. But music? Same-o, same-o. Same notes, same instruments. Today we'll break out into a new era. ARE YOU READY?" he shouted.

Scattered applause greeted him. With a flourish, Woody switched on the Apple and Korg, then toggled "play."

Angie, standing alongside, studied the audience as the first musical phrase belched from the speakers. Woody, arms akimbo, gazed expectantly at the crowd, which stirred and murmured amongst themselves. Woody's song reverberated across the courtyard, rising in intensity while the audience grumbled. Abruptly, a group of four students rose and walked out. They were followed by two more and then dozens. By the time

Woody played the second song, most of the gathering had left. As the last song finished, a smattering of die-hards, including the department chair, shrugged and stalked away. No applause, just shaking heads.

Stunned, Woody turned to Angie. Tears were streaming down her cheeks.

"What happened?" Woody stammered. "Why?"

"They just weren't ready to move past the old stuff. You're too advanced." She blotted her eyes on the sleeve of her blouse. "I'm sorry, Woody. I know how hard you worked. Putting a computer together with a synth is a super idea, so maybe we could work on more songs—songs that are more melodic or something. What do you say?"

Wordlessly, Woody packed the equipment into boxes and lugged them to his car while Angie helped two music students return the amplifier and speakers to storage.

The drive back to *Angie's Raft* passed without a word. Woody parked, stepped from the car, and headed directly toward the yacht.

"Hey! Don't you want to take your equipment aboard?" shouted Angie.

He waved his hand dismissively and disappeared down the hatch.

With a shrug, Angie locked the paraphernalia in the car and followed Woody. She found him sitting glumly on the sofa, staring into space. She dropped beside him and took his hand. "Bad day, huh?"

Slowly his gaze turned to her. "Bad day? Not really—just totally fucked up."

Jolted by his newfound vulgarity, she rubbed his arm with affection. "I remember what my parents said about rock and roll. 'Trash,' they said. 'It'll never go anywhere.' Look what happened. Maybe your music will go the same way. It's *so* different that listeners might need a little time to appreciate it."

With a passive look on his face, Woody said nothing.

"Want to start working on a few fresh songs? With your imagination, we could compose something a little more conventional while still keeping the Apple-Korg thing. What do you say?"

Silence.

They sat for a time not speaking. Finally, Angie said, "How about a bite to eat? It's dinnertime and you must be starving." Without waiting for an answer, she walked to the galley and boiled some hotdogs. After slathering the buns with mustard, she sprinkled them with diced onions. Angie spooned a glob of grocery store potato salad on the plate and, after pulling two beers from the refrigerator, she called out, "It's ready."

With a heavy sigh, Woody came to the table and picked at his food.

"Come on. Eat up. This is one of your favorites."

"Not hungry." He finished off his beer and went to get another.

Pretending nothing was amiss, Angie cleared the table and rinsed the dishes.

Woody didn't budge for an hour except for another trip to the refrigerator. Now, he sat with his head in his hands, two empty beer cans in front of him, and a cold one by his elbow.

"You going to just sit there and get plastered?" Angie walked over and began massaging Woody's shoulders. "Feel good?"

"Hmm."

She leaned over and kissed his ear. "Feel good?"

"Hmmm."

"You know what would really feel good?" She kissed his neck and rubbed her breast on his arm. "Really, really good?" She reached over and rubbed his thigh.

"Hmmmmm."

Moments later in bed, Woody discovered he couldn't perform in spite of their usually raucous sex life.

Blushing with embarrassment, he bolted upright in bed and shouted, "I hate music!"

* * *

Despondent, Woody tried to keep his grades up, but the specter of the concert disaster scrambled all efforts to study. Things were further complicated when Angie's parents came back from vacation and began frequent outings on their yacht, so attempts to reestablish their relationship sputtered. Trying to help out, Angie scheduled music lessons in a nearby park or in the library, but Woody couldn't concentrate.

One afternoon, Angie announced, "I can't study with you today as we planned because I have a new job."

"A job?"

"Well, not a real job. I'm volunteering for the Yale Symphony Orchestra. I'll be setting up chairs and music stands. That sort of thing. The best part is they want me to organize sheet music and make sure every musician has the right part. Even the conductor's score. Exciting, huh?"

"Sure, sounds great," he droned.

With the boat taken over by her parents and Angie's increasing absences at the orchestra, Woody sank into an alcoholic morass. Whisky replaced beer and morning headaches became common while his roommate greeted him every day with a scowl of disgust and demanded he stay away from his belongings. That became a real problem because Woody had been using his roommate's Play Station to dabble in Pac-Man or Rogue. In response, Woody dipped into his allowance and bought his own game console. Soon addicted to computer games, classroom attendance steadily declined, as did his grades.

When he stopped shaving and bathing, Angie grabbed him by the collar and screamed, "What the crap is the matter with you? You trying to kill yourself? I'm about ready to split—leave you to your own devices. You hear?"

* * *

The next morning, freshly showered and shaven, Woody waited for Angie outside the music building. Four aspirin tablets had tamped down his headache, but the bright sun still hurt his bloodshot eyes. Impatiently, he searched the steps coming from the classrooms, shifting from foot to foot, and looking for Angie.

At last, she appeared chatting with a guy carrying a violin case. *Who's he? She seems awfully interested in what he's saying. He looks like a senior, all sophisticated.*

They were about to walk past when Angie noticed Woody. She shifted her eyes back to her friend and they started to walk away. But then, she said something to him and turned back to Woody. The violin guy kept walking.

"Well, at least you don't look like the wrath of God this morning. I guess you want to talk?"

He nodded. "I know I've been a jerk, but I couldn't help it. It's the Korg thing that has me down. Those three songs meant the world to me."

"I know. Let's find that bench where we first met. We'll talk."

Shyly, Woody slipped his hand into Angie's and was rewarded with a tiny smile. As they walked, he tried to put the violin guy out of his mind, but had to ask, "Who's the fellow you were walking with?"

"Chuck? He's a teaching assistant for my music theory class." She snickered to herself. "Nice guy, but not to worry; he's engaged."

"Oh, it's nothing, I was just curious," Woody lied. "Is this our bench?" he asked.

"Woodrow Sterling Lawrence, are you telling me you don't remember? That tells me how little you think of our relationship."

"Don't get mad. Now that I look closely, I see it is," he lied, hoping it was. Mercifully, his luck held.

They sat down; Angie crossed her legs and turned toward him. "All right, I want you to tell me what's going on. You've become a total ass since our concert. You going to class?"

"Not much."

"You've decided to flunk out?"

"Not really."

Angie poked Woody on the chest with her finger. "Look, you jerk, you gotta *talk* to me. Explain yourself! These one or two-word utterances aren't going to hack it."

Ashamed, Woody stared at the ground. "It's just I'm not sure what I'm doing. Father wants me to be a lawyer, but the thought makes me want to puke. My mother has bailed out on me. I love computers, but suddenly, they have competition."

"Competition?"

"Yeah. You did it to me, you know. First it was Billy Joel and the music lessons you gave me. Once I thought that science was everything, but now I see music might bring a bit of magic into my life. I was really convinced my songs were special. I guess they turned out especially bad." He rubbed his temples and thought back to matchstick rockets and all the other aborted attempts at fame and fortune. "I seem to have this habit of getting all excited about something and then screwing it up, like the Korg fiasco. Suddenly, I'm afraid to try anything."

Angie reached over and hugged him. "Do you know why I love you? It's your enthusiasm, your willingness to try wild things. Most people go through life in a sodden daze. They have no ambition, no zeal for life. Not you, Woody! Yup, you flunked 'Concert 101' but so what? Who but you would have even tried?"

"Guess I *am* kinda crazy," Woody grinned. "But right now, I'm tired, just tired. Maybe I need to find a new direction. I'm twenty years old and a sophomore at Yale and you'd think I'd know where my life is going by now."

Angie kissed him lightly on the cheek. "Tell you what, my folks are away on business for two days, so the yacht is ours. Let's gather up a toothbrush and the usual stuff and spend the night. I bought a couple of new records for a school assignment, so maybe we could listen to a little music. What do you say?"

"Just music?" leered Woody.

* * *

The euphoria of rousing sex lingered. The incoming tide set the hawsers creaking with strain and gulls shrieked at one another. Angie turned to Woody and said, "Welcome back."

He pulled her to him and kissed her lightly. "Glad to be back."

With a contented sigh, Angie slipped from bed. "I think there's a bag of Fritos in our grocery bag. That will have to do for dinner unless you want to go over to the restaurant."

"Whatever you want, my love."

"Let's stay aboard. We bought a bottle of wine and I want to play a record or two for you. Remember?"

"My pounding head tells me to limit myself to just one glass of wine; not sure about any music." Thoughts of "The Concert" made him shudder.

"You just listen to the wrong kind of music. I have something special."

"Not synthesizer music I hope."

Angie laughed. "No, silly. I'm talking about *good* music." She ripped open the Fritos and poured two glasses of wine. "Sit," she commanded.

Wearing only his shorts, Woody dropped on the couch and took a handful of Fritos. "Good," he proclaimed. His face wrinkled when he sipped the wine. "Chips and Chardonnay don't mix."

"So now you're a friggin' gourmet?" Angie quipped. She walked to the record player and pulled a record from its sleeve. With a grin, she said, "You ready?"

"So who is it? More Billy Joel? Maybe Blondie? Pink Floyd?"

"None of that. Something very different. Take it from your friendly music-major, this will burrow into your very soul. It will sweep away the clouds in your life."

Woody grinned. "Well, I'm ready for something new. Ready to leave all that old stuff behind, including those Korg-clouds."

Angie gently set the phonograph needle on the record and delicate violins filled the cabin with melody. Surprised, Woody scowled. "What's this?"

"Shhhh," scolded Angie, holding a finger to her lips. "Beethoven," she whispered. "Now be quiet."

Skeptical, Woody leaned back and crossed his arms. He didn't recognize all the instruments, but voices of a flute and oboe soared while bassoons moaned. Soon, horns and clarinets picked up the melody and the music danced across Woody's consciousness. After a pause, the symphony began once more with a swaying mellow tempo.

"Do you hear the cuckoo bird?" whispered Angie.

Surprised, Woody nodded. "Yeah."

Then horns, trumpets and drums crashed and banged bringing Woody upright. "What the hell?"

"Shhhh."

Soon, the music softened and Woody relaxed, his foot slowly tapping out the tempo. The music ended and Angie switched off the player. "Well, what do you think?"

"You're right. I've never heard anything like this. Not half bad. You called it Bay…"

"Beethoven. His Sixth Symphony. It's called the Pastoral. He composed it about 170 years ago when he was nearly deaf."

"You're kidding! How can a deaf guy write music if he can't hear it?"

"The music was in his heart, not his ears. He liked to take long walks in the woods hoping the quiet would help his hearing. Did you think his symphony sounded like a walk in the woods?"

Woody rubbed his chin. "Could have, I guess."

"I'm going to play it again. It starts with Beethoven walking into a serene forest, and then listening to a brook. That's where the cuckoo bird was. Next, a storm breaks up a party of country peasants, but it passes and the fun starts up again. Got it?"

"The storm is where it got loud, right?"

"See? You're already part way there." She played the record again.

The yacht disappeared and Woody strolled in a forest. A birdcall harmonized with a gurgling stream until a torrent of rain and crashing thunder invaded his peaceful reverie. Finally, tranquility returned and Woody smiled. "Wow, that is something. It sounded really complicated. How many musicians in an orchestra?"

"Oh, it depends. For a Beethoven symphony, maybe eighty or a hundred."

"A hundred?" Woody shook his head. "I heard a bunch of different instruments, right? It seemed like they're all playing different tunes. Weird."

"When we've more time, I'll explain the various instruments and a thing called counterpoint. But what I want to know is what did you think about Beethoven?"

Woody thoughtfully tapped his chin with a fist. "You know, it beats a computerized Korg going away. Beethoven's Sixth Symphony? I guess he composed others."

"Sure did. So did Haydn and Mozart. Wanna hear more?"

"You bet. You have a convert."

* * *

The blast of a fog horn jolted Woody from his sleep. He squinted through a porthole and saw nothing but gray. Angie, already awake, rattled dishes in the galley while humming a tune.

"Is that a Beethoven symphony you're singing?" Woody called out, jokingly.

Laughing, she replied, "Actually it is, but not the Sixth. The Yale orchestra is rehearsing the Third Symphony, so it's on my mind. This morning I have to help set up for a performance. We better clean up everything quickly—can't leave a trace that we were here. We can't forget the grocery bags we brought."

"I guess I'd better get a move on." He struggled from bed and dressed. He sidled up to Angie and kissed her passionately.

"Hey, we don't have time for that." She wiped off the counter and hung the towel back where she found it. "This concert is a big production. The stage has to be set up, flyers have to be delivered to stores downtown, posters put up around campus, all kinds of stuff. I'll jam everything in between classes. I'll probably spend most of the day there. I'm really excited about it."

"You sure spend a lot of time volunteering for them. When is the performance?"

"Just two days from now. It's a damned panic time for sure." She tipped her head to one side and tapped his arm. "You have class this morning?" she asked mischievously.

"Not until one."

"Here's an idea. Why don't you come with me and help? Now that you're a new-born symphony nut, you can get the inside dope."

Woody scowled. "I've never been to that kind of concert. I bet they don't even have a mosh pit. I wouldn't know what to do."

"You don't have to play first violin, dummy. You can help set up chairs, music stands, that sort of thing. You know—strong back, weak mind."

"Well, I don't know."

Angie painted her face with a pleading little girl expression and said, "Pretty please? Just for me?"

With a chuckle, Woody gave her a big hug. "You know I can't resist you, even if you're selling me into slave labor."

Together they briskly finished cleaning *Angie's Raft* and scurried to the car. After a quick breakfast at McDonald's, they hurried through the backstage door at the concert hall. Woody's mouth gaped at the sight. The vast cavern of the hall had soaring pillars that reached beyond elaborate balconies up to an elegant vault. Organ pipes formed the backdrop to the stage, which swarmed with stagehands and student volunteers. Row upon row of stark lights dotted the distant ceiling, spattering puddles of light on the stage. Two young men tugged an immense black drape across the back of the stage while two more pushed a piano into the wings.

"Before you get involved, let me introduce you to the orchestra's manager," Angie said, her eyes searching the area. "There he is, over by the lighting booth. Come on."

They waited a few moments as the manager finished a conversation with a technician. "Sam, I'd like you to meet my boyfriend, Woody Lawrence. Woody this is Samuel Richter."

"Everyone just calls me Sam," he chuckled. "Are you here to help Angie?"

"If I want to remain her boyfriend."

"It sounds like you understand the male role of survival," Sam laughed.

With a wave to Sam, Woody and Angie walked out onto the stage. "Woody, grab those music stands over there and put them where the tape on the floor marks their position," Awkwardly, he lugged two stands and set them on their marks. "No, no. They face the other way," Angie cried out.

He dodged a dolly loaded with a collapsible platform, which turned out to be the conductor's podium. Another crew erected more risers toward the back of the stage. Angie breezed by with an armload of sheet music and pointed, "Those platforms way back there are for timpani. You'd call them drums. Clarinets and bassoons are closer. You'll see."

Woody's mind whirled. He'd never seen such intense activity. He fought two, even three music stands at a time and set them on the tape with all the precision he could muster. Thinking he'd nearly finished; he saw the stagehands building another level of risers. *More tape.* Out of breath, he ran for more music stands.

A while later, Angie dashed by pointing at her watch, "Time for your class!" she yelled. "Better get going."

Feeling a mixture of disappointment and relief, Woody fled the scene.

* * *

That evening they met at Lillie's Cafe for dinner. Angie set two tickets for the performance of the Third Symphony on the table. "I used my womanly charm to get a hold of these. There's a catch, though, I promised you would help out again tomorrow."

"No problem! Working there is a lot of fun, even if my back is killin' me."

"I knew I could count on you." She snatched a napkin and pulled out a pencil from her purse. "Let's compare our class schedules for tomorrow to see when we could meet. Okay, what do you have going?"

"Why don't I cut classes tomorrow and spend the day helping you?"

"Woody, you have to stay on top of your school work."

"That's what my father is always saying, but why should my life's goal be law school? I'm not learning anything useful. Take my political science class for example; it's about election laws and international governments. Who cares about communism in Cuba?"

Angie's frightful glare silenced Woody. "Yeah, I know." He fiddled with his meal, twisting a ball of spaghetti on the fork. "Is Beethoven's Third as good as the Sixth?"

"You're changing the subject," Angie growled.

"Well?"

"I think it is every bit as good, but it's different. You'll love it." She rapped the pencil on the table rapidly like a machine gun. "Now, tell me when your classes are."

The next night they walked out after the performance and Angie's prediction had hit the mark; Woody was mesmerized. "Those first two notes really jumped out at me," he said. "Nearly wet my pants. Sure different than the other one. It had a lot of energy. The music went from really quiet to blasting away. All those weird looking instruments." He chuckled, remembering his research on the oboe. "You promised to tell me all about them."

"I'll try to find time, but the end of the term is coming up and that means final exams. Besides the orchestra is planning two more concerts, so I'll be damned busy with them."

As the next two weeks tumbled by, Woody found himself in the clutches of the Yale Orchestra. The production crew discovered his technical skills and sought his help with audio and lighting in addition to schlepping music stands. They had a piano concerto one night and a soprano soloist the next, requiring completely different preparations. Woody basked in the variety and the challenges. He cut poly sci once more to help put gels on the overhead lights.

No surprise, he failed the course and the university put him on probation.

* * *

"Woodrow," bellowed his father into the telephone. "What's this notice from the university about probation? 'Failure to make up for the 'F' will result in dismissal,' it says."

His father's shouts were so loud, Woody had to hold the receiver away from his ear. "Yes, I know, father. I just got too busy. No problem, though. I'll make it up for sure."

"Too busy? Too busy with that girl? With concerts like you told me about? You're not motivated, that's what. You need an incentive to get in gear, so I'll give you one."

Woody's chest tightened.

"Your allowance just went to zero, Woodrow. No more eating out—it's brown bag time. No more concerts. Library duty instead. If you need a couple of bucks, you call me and explain why. Got it?"

* * *

"I see you're bombed out of your mind again, Woody. I've had it. I'm going to petition the Residential College administrators for a different roommate. I'm not wasting another two years with you."

"Thass fine. You go ahead." Not bothering with a glass, Woody took another swig straight from the bourbon bottle. He sank lower in the chair and stared at his feet, ignoring his roommate.

Two days had passed since the phone call with his father and Woody hadn't seen a sober moment. He begged off a dinner date with Angie, claiming he had the flu. Oblivion suited him just fine.

Worried, Angie went to Woody's dorm the next morning and called from the lobby. Getting no answer, she phoned the infirmary to see if he had checked in. When she found out he wasn't there, Angie returned to the dorm and asked at the desk if someone would go up and check on him. The clerk came down shortly with a sheepish look on his face. "Seems like he's drunk. Passed out."

More concerned than mad, she kept calling and finally got a hold of him late that afternoon. "You've been drinking again, Woody. What's going on?"

"How'd you find out? Oh, never mind." He held back a groan. "I flunked poly sci and had a big fight with father. I'm in serious trouble."

"You should have known, Woody. You've been cutting classes right and left. I don't know why I put up with you. First, you flunk a class and your answer to that problem is to get blasted? If you want me in your life, we'd better damn well work this out."

"Not tonight, Angie. I feel like I'm at a turning point in my life, but my brain has crashed. I need a little time to decide what's next, okay? Why don't we connect tomorrow?"

"Your damn brain didn't crash; it's pickled," Angie snarled. "You going to get drunk again?"

After a long pause, Woody said, "No, I don't think so. Some poet wrote something about two roads and I'm looking at them. Maybe there are ten roads; I'm not sure. Regardless, it's time I decide what to do with my life and all I know for certain is I'm no lawyer."

Miffed, Angie said, "Okay, I'll be at the concert hall helping to clean up. If you have sorted out your life by afternoon, give me a call."

* * *

A hint of dawn cast a glow on the empty bed of his ex-roommate. Woody rubbed his eyes, red from a sleepless night. He had come to two major decisions: he was tired of fighting with his father and he was tired of Yale. He had only a week left to enroll in summer's make-up class, but the deadline had no meaning. He would drop out of school and get a job.

In spite of the early hour, he picked up the phone and dialed his father.

A groggy voice answered, "Hello?"

"Father, it's me, Woody. Not Woodrow, just Woody."

"Do you know what time it is?"

"Sure do. It's time to tell you I'm not going to be a lawyer. Time to say I'm not going back to school. I'm going to get a job."

"Are you nuts? What kind of job do you think you can get without a degree? You could flush your entire future down the toilet! You have to stick with the plan! Am I clear?"

"Very, but Yale is on the wrong road. I'm getting a job."

"Road? What road are you talking about? You quit the University and I'll disown you. You'll not get a penny! Am…I…clear?"

"Very." Woody took a deep breath. "I'll get a job."

"Crap!" There was a click on the phone and Woody grinned.

"That's step one."

* * *

On the second ring, Angie picked up. "Hello?"

"It's me. You ready for a super serious conversation this afternoon?"

"Ah-hah. Has the wandering student discovered the course of his life?" Angie said with a snide tone in her voice.

"Working on it. Meet at Lillie's?"

Secretly relieved, Angie agreed. "Give me twenty minutes."

The stifling summer heat hammered Angie as she trudged to the rendezvous. Breathless, she slipped into the booth opposite Woody, snatched a napkin, and blotted her forehead. "Whew, I trust your revelations will make my damned sweat worthwhile." With a critical eye, she studied Woody. "You seem sober; good for you. However, your eyes are the color of a stop sign; get any sleep?"

"None at all. Too busy thinking." A nervous flutter jiggled Woody's stomach. "The key realization I had last night was that I'm tired. Ever try to excel at something when you're totally washed out? So, I finally figured out that I'm really tired about two things."

The waitress came and took their orders, leaving Angie curious.

"You were saying?"

"Tired. I decided I'm done with my father and his lawyer fixation. I called him and told him so."

"Wow! What did he say to that?"

"Not much. He disowned me."

Angie choked on her Coke. "That's a disaster! He's worth millions!"

"Maybe, but my life isn't for sale. You've known all along how I've fought over his lawyer business." He leaned back and smiled. "Not a problem anymore."

Shaking her head, Angie said, "You mentioned there are two things. Dare I ask what is the second?"

Woody took Angie's hand. "You ready?"

"No, but tell me anyway."

"I'm quitting Yale."

Angie blanched. "Quitting? You can't! You have two years invested. You're halfway there!"

"Not if you count grad school," he corrected. "I ask myself, 'What have I learned?' Hardly anything except from your talks about music and volunteering at the orchestra. All my classes were aimed at law school. Nothing stuck." He shrugged. "No father and no Yale. I'm on a new road."

Angie tried to sort through her thoughts. "So where is this strange road going to take you?"

"I'm going to get a job. I spent most the morning looking through the want ads. Lots going on."

Incredulous, Angie couldn't believe what she heard. "A job? What kind of job can a goddamned college dropout get?" she snapped. "The legendary burger-flipping job? Perhaps bagging groceries? What happened to the all those big dreams you cherished?"

"Simmer down will you? I'll find a job that will be a foundation for big things. Steve Jobs started puttering in his garage and look what happened. Just give me a little time."

Angie couldn't decide if she should throw the saltshaker at him or give him a hug. She'd known of his struggles all along and had tried to help him, but things hadn't improved. Time and again he found solace in alcohol. Sure, he'd jumped into the music thing and enjoyed volunteering with the orchestra, but where could that go? Across the table, Woody's eyes glittered with adventure and his broad smile invited her understanding. Abruptly, she stood, slid over on the bench seat next to Woody, and gave him a big kiss.

* * *

The Sunday newspaper listed three pages of job openings and Woody lined up four interviews, none of which turned out to be the "foundation for big things." Disappointed, but not defeated, he decided to spend the last of his shrinking allowance money on a record of another Beethoven symphony. As he walked through the door of the A-Sharp music store, he saw a sign in the window. "Help Wanted."

Mulling over the sign, his thoughts were interrupted by a clerk. "May I help you?"

"What? Oh, yeah. I'd like a record of Beethoven's best ever symphony. What would you recommend?"

"Beethoven? We don't get much call for him," the young lady laughed. "I'll guess that his best seller is the Fifth Symphony, but a lot of customers like the Ninth better."

"I'm stumped. Should I go with the crowd or your recommendation? How about his Tenth or Twenty-First?"

"He only wrote nine, silly. The Ninth is the one with singing. It's called the Choral."

"Well, I like singing, so I'll take that one." As she was ringing up the sale, Woody's mind returned to the sign in the window. "What's with the help wanted sign?"

"You'll have to talk with the manager about that. It's something about the new computer he bought and inventory control." She shrugged and handed him the L.P.

Woody's mental antenna swiveled in her direction. *Computers?* "The manager? Is he here?"

"In the back. You looking for work?"

"Yeah, sure am. I'm good with computers."

"Follow me."

The back office overflowed with musical instruments, catalogs, and debris of all kinds. Hidden in the back, a balding, overweight, middle-age man hunched behind a scarred desk.

"Randy, this guy is looking for a job. Wanna talk to him?" the clerk asked. "Says he's good with computers."

The manager looked up. "You know computers?" he asked, waving at a dust covered Apple II on a table behind him.

"Yup. Sure do."

"I got suckered in by the best salesman I've ever seen. Told me that thing can do payroll, inventory, place orders-everything. So far, all I can get it to do is hold down that table."

Woody set aside a pile of paper on the side chair, clutched his new record to his chest, and sat. "You are in luck, Randy. That machine will do everything you mentioned and more, and I'm the guy who can make it sing close harmony."

"You sound slicker than the bastard who sold it to me. You're going to have to prove it."

Woody slid his chair over to the computer. "Watch this."

That evening he called Angie. "I've got a job stocking shelves and sweeping the floor! Pay isn't much but here's the big news! I'll also be putting an

Apple online for the A—Sharp music store, part of a nationwide chain called Abbott Associates. That's one more step down the road to fame. Let's celebrate with a big dinner, okay?" He gulped. "You'll have to pay. I'm broke."

* * *

They settled into a fresh routine: Woody learning the ropes at work and Angie attending summer session. Yale's orchestra flew off on a tour to Great Britain and Ireland, which required travel arrangements and preparation of myriad musical instruments for shipment. Woody found himself helping to book flights and hotels, even nailing crates together for the instruments. Trips to the yacht slacked off because Angie's parents cruised almost every weekend, but weeknight forays continued even though Angie suspected her folks were on to them.

Late July found Woody bubbling with enthusiasm about his job. He cornered Angie and said, "Randy, that's my boss, can't believe what I've done with the Apple. I just finished setting up a program for inventory control and ordering of stock. He can't believe how slick it is. Want the good news?"

Angie nodded.

"He gave me a raise! Told me to focus on the computer—he'll stock the shelves at night! He wants me to look into the sales angle to see if we could build it up. There's no limit!"

The calendar swept them into the fall and Woody managed to find time to work with the orchestra in the evenings. He had talked Sam into buying an Apple II for the orchestra and programmed it to track schedules, ticket sales, and contracts with soloists. Impressed, the stage manager assigned two student helpers to Woody, speeding along audio and lighting setups. To Randy's delight, Woody began suggesting that the performers go to the A—Sharp music store for new instruments, supplies, and maintenance.

Angie rejoiced in Woody's pursuit of a "foundation for big things" and as an aside, explained the difference between a violin and a viola. Their relationship flourished.

The Herald American
Tuesday, January 11, 1983
Section B1: Business News

Unemployment Remains High

The New Year Begins with Ten Percent Out of Work

Three years passed and Woody had been promoted to assistant manager of the music store. A trickle of customers from the Yale Orchestra triggered an idea in Woody's mind. Musicians required corks and pads for woodwinds and valve replacement for horns. Not to mention tuning for pianos. Slowly, he created a side business for Randy's store: major repair of instruments. On Woody's insistence, the store began selling "instrument health insurance" policies to fund future maintenance needs, discounted of course, for Yale students. He replaced the old Apple II in favor of the new Apple Lisa, which Woody programmed to track warranty claims and customer buying habits. Sales crept higher. Keeping true to his nature, Woody sprinted wildly through the days, untouched by rampant nationwide unemployment.

Angie graduated with honors and took a position teaching music theory and piano at the nearby Gateway Community College, one of the few jobs available. They pooled their funds and rented a modest apartment conveniently located halfway between their respective jobs. The need of *Angie's Raft* died except on occasional weekend fishing trips with her parents.

Woody jockeyed the abandoned Apple II computer from A—Sharp onto a card table in the bedroom while Angie looked on, shaking her head. "Just because Randy gave you the thing for nothing, doesn't mean you have to piddle around with the damn thing."

With a grunt, Woody set the monitor on top of the CPU. "I came up with a super-hot idea for a sales and marketing program. Not just for A—Sharp, but for Abbott's whole network of stores. I bet I can double their sales within a year or two."

"But you said the Lisa is much better."

"No matter, I can make them talk to one another. I can't concentrate at the store—customers running in and out asking questions all the time. Here, it's quiet."

"Set that aside for now," Angie said with a stern voice. "You promised we'd paint the dining nook and there's pictures to hang."

Woody pouted. "I guess my idea can wait."

And so that spring they settled into their new home, trying hand-me-down furniture in different spots and hanging cheap curtains. Late nights found Woody hunched over his computer while Angie prepped her lecture notes. All contact with Woody's father ceased. Even though their lives became hectic, warmth washed over their personal relationship. Angie nearly swooned with joy when Woody presented her with a tiny stuffed kitten with big glass eyes on Valentine's Day.

One early summer afternoon, Woody tapped on the computer keyboard and suddenly whooped, "That's it! It's done! Wait until Randy sees this; his sales will blast off!"

"Already?" Angie called out from the kitchen. "Didn't take all that long."

The next morning Woody lugged the Apple II into work and patched it into the Lisa. After downloading his new sales and marketing program, he methodically checked it out. After a couple of tweaks, he yelled, "Randy, come see this!"

With one of those "here we go again looks" Randy sat beside Woody.

"See this message? Says "Big Sale On Guitars."

"Yeah, so what?"

"I can send it to hundreds, even thousands of people with a click of this button." Squirming with excitement, Woody said, "A while back they came up with this thing called CompuServe. It's a program for IBM computers, but I figured a way to adapt it for Apples. Give a phone call to Yale's orchestra office. Ask them to look at their computer."

"What are you talking about?"

"Just do it."

It took a little coaching, but shortly Randy turned to Woody with a surprised look, "They can see the message about the guitar. How in the world…?"

"You can start shopping for that Corvette you've always wanted. With this computer, I'll have sales take off faster than the space shuttle."

And so it did. Within a month, stock to fill the flurry of orders swamped the back room and overflowed into the front sales floor.

"This is fantastic," Randy said. "I can't keep up with the demand. I figure to take out a loan to add an extension to the place with conveyors, shelving, the works." He thumped Woody on the back. "From now on, you're the manager of sales and marketing."

"I have a better idea," Woody exclaimed. "We have a fantastic track record, so why don't we sell Abbott's corporate headquarters on the idea? You could become their big deal vice president and I'd take over A—Sharp. What do you say?"

"I like your style."

Woody put together a proposal for Abbott, explaining the potential of CompuServe shopping and the workings of his program. He included tabulations of the sales growth at A—Sharp and projected future revenues. Randy admitted the package was impressive, and sent it in.

Other than a terse note saying they'd received the proposal, no other communication from corporate offices occurred. After a week, Woody became antsy. "What's with those guys? Give them a call, Randy. Ask what's the big delay."

"Well, I don't want to appear pushy, but I'll give them a buzz tomorrow."

The next morning, Randy walked up to Woody. "Something weird is going on at Corporate. All they'll tell me is some changes are happening. Guess we sit tight for a while. In the meantime, I'll push to finish our new building expansion."

A month passed without word until a registered letter arrived. "Abbott and Associates Inc. have been purchased by a conglomerate to be named shortly. The new owner has highly sophisticated programs for their mainframe computer including sales. In light of these events, Abbott has no use for the sales and marketing software offered by A—Sharp. More information will be forthcoming soon."

Ultimately, the ax fell. All business activities had to conform to the new owner's stringent procedures. Resources would be consolidated and strict cost-saving measures imposed. Woody's program became obsolete, obliterated by the immense corporate IBM mainframe. Sales at A—Sharp plummeted because use of Woody's new program was prohibited pending further instructions.

"I don't know how I can hang on," moaned Randy. "I took out a big loan to build the addition and buy equipment we no longer need. If I could, I'd buy A—Sharp myself, but I don't have the money. Damn, we had a good thing going, Woody." He wrung his hands in misery.

Dumbfounded, Woody's vision of conquering the music world vanished. "It's the matchstick rockets and the Korg catastrophes all over again," he mumbled.

"What?"

"Nothing."

* * *

Randy managed to hold on for two months and then sold the store to a retail book outlet. There was barely enough money to pay off Randy's loan. Looking gray and defeated, he moved to Atlanta to live with his daughter.

Prodded by Angie, Woody looked for work and finally hired into a financial firm doing data entry. The pay was a fraction of A—Sharp's and the job so boring he had trouble staying awake. *Lucky to have any kind of job, I guess.* Despondency settled on his shoulders like a massive overcoat. *There's nothing more that can go wrong,* he thought.

Woody's gloom weighed on Angie too. She'd tried to cheer him up and constantly searched the newspaper hoping to find rewarding work for Woody, but with little luck. She had hoped to find an inexpensive piano so she could start giving private lessons, but their sudden poverty precluded such things, dragging her spirits further down.

All in all, moroseness and darkness seeped through the windows and flooded the little house. They rarely spoke and made love even less.

Late one chilly November evening, Woody dragged himself home and collapsed on the couch. "Made a few errors today. The boss is on my case. I can't focus on all that trivia."

Angie sat next to him and took his hand.

Woody, seeing her serious expression, asked, "What?"

She took a deep breath. "I'm pregnant."

The words nearly strangled him. "No way! You're on the pill!"

"Well, maybe I missed a day or two."

"You sure you're pregnant?"

"Positive."

Woody slumped further. "There's no money. We're hardly getting by as it is." He wrung his hands. "There's no way we can manage a baby right now."

"You're not suggesting an abortion, are you?"

He jerked to his feet and paced. "What are the alternatives, Angie?"

"I don't know. Maybe your father could help?"

"No way!" Woody shouted. "He's out of my life for good! Haven't talked to him in ages!"

"My folks might be able to help. They're tight-lipped about their finances and it took considerable loot to put me through school, but I'm sure they'd pitch in. After all, they have a big yacht and all."

Indignant, Woody growled, "I wouldn't take their money if they had it. I stand on my own feet!"

They stared at each other silently for a long time. Finally, Angie said, "I'm not having an abortion. This is *our* child. We'll find a way."

Woody stormed out of the house shouting, "I need a drink."

They fought bitterly over the next month, getting more and more vicious with one another. One day in a rage, Woody screamed, "This is going nowhere! I'm outta here." He threw some clothes and his toothbrush into an old suitcase and drove off in the car. Angie watched him leave with tears streaming down her cheeks.

Shaking in anger, he bought a bottle of cheap bourbon and checked into a motel. The next morning, with a pounding head, he managed to show up for work. Stunned by the cost of the motel, that night he found a parking spot behind a department store and crawled into the back seat to sleep.

Angie, after depositing her breakfast into the toilet, called a colleague, and hitched a ride to school. *I'll find a way, with or without him.*

* * *

Because Woody ran off with their car, Angie's most immediate problem was transportation. The solution quickly appeared when Jim, another teacher at Gateway, overheard her asking for a ride to her place. "Car in the shop?" he asked.

"No. I broke up with my boyfriend and he took the car."

"Nice guy, huh?" A wide smile stretched across his face. "Well now, your troubles are over. I'll open up 'Jim's Taxi Service,' just for you."

"Oh I couldn't impose. Besides your fiancé might get suspicious."

"Betty? She'll understand. You're a colleague in a bind, that's all."

After a few weeks, while driving her home, Jim lightly poked her stomach. "Puttin' on a little weight, Angie?"

"You might say that." Clenching her jaw, she continued. "I'm pregnant—about twelve weeks along."

"Wow! And your boyfriend has taken a powder. What are you going to do?"

"Going through with it."

"Your call. Let me know if I can help. Drive you to the doctor, go grocery shopping, whatever. I bet Betty would lend a hand too."

* * *

In the meantime, Woody struggled with a terrible job, self-doubt, but mostly about Angie. *I knocked her up. No, she should have been more careful with the pill. Do I have the guts to kill a baby? Is it really a baby by now? If I don't take care of Angie and the baby, what will she do? Heard through the grapevine she's dating that teacher. Is it getting serious?* Disgusted, he clenched his fists. *I'm such a turd leaving her stranded. What am I going to do?*

To prove his manliness and independence, he dated a girl twice, but compared to Angie she was a dud. At work, the boss gave him a written warning: "Improve your performance or you'll be terminated."

The old visions of matchstick rockets, space shuttle models, and his spreadsheet plagued his dreams. A particularly vivid nightmare about a computer rejecting his attempts at data entry woke him in a sweat. Shaking, he stumbled from bed and reached for the bourbon bottle. Staring at it, he thought, *No, this isn't the answer. I can do big things, great things. Maybe first I should try being a father.*

That morning, he called Angie.

The Herald American
Thursday, August 17, 1984
Section C2: Technology Today

NASA Launches AMPTE

Three Space Craft to Seek Solar Wind

Longing for the good old days of Apollo and moon landings, Woody found things like AMPTE exceptionally boring. He peeked over his newspaper and watched Angie walk down the hall. Her immense size changed her normally light-footed gait into a ponderous waddle. At mealtime, she had to turn sideways because her belly wedged her away from the table. For the same reason, she could no longer drive, so Woody joyfully took over as chauffeur.

Frequent discussions failed to come up with a name for the baby. At night in bed, Woody always rested his hand on her tummy, laughing every time the baby-to-be kicked. Scientific–like, he taped a calendar on the wall and drew bold X's on the passing days: 19, 18, 17… "It brings back the good old Apollo countdowns," he chuckled. Together, they poured over pamphlets from the pediatrician's office and read "How-To" books on childbirth. Woody lavished Angie with a combination of his inbred logic and profound affection, plus he presented her with another furry stuffed kitten with big eyes. She reveled in it.

On the night of day six, Angie eased into bed complaining, "My back really aches, but I don't want to take an aspirin. Just deal with it, I guess."

"I can give you a back-rub," Woody offered.

"No way. I can't lie on my stomach. Anyway, it's not all that bad."

Dawn peeked through the gap in the drapes when Angie woke Woody. "I might be having contractions and I think my water broke. I'm a mess."

Instantly wide-awake, Woody sprang from bed. "Wow! It's starting! Let's get you cleaned up."

Dressed in a warm bathrobe and house slippers, Angie sat on the sofa looking anxious. Woody perched alongside with a clipboard and pencil. When Angie grunted softly, he asked, "Another one?" He looked at his watch.

Angie nodded and then breathed easily. "Yes. They're getting stronger."

"That was sixteen minutes." He jotted the figure on the clipboard.

With a chuckle, Angie said, "You're not at all like a true computer nerd. Damn paper-and-pencil? Really?"

Waving the pencil, he quipped, "I don't have to plug it in."

True to form, Woody documented the countdown. Thirteen minutes, eleven minutes. The hours dragged by. Between labor pains, Angie walked around the living room on Woody's arm. As the contractions became sharper, her whimpers became moans.

"Nine and a half minutes, I think it's time to head to the hospital," Woody said, his voice shaking.

"I'm more than ready," Angie said, wincing with another pain.

He guided her down the porch steps, carrying her overnight bag they'd packed months ago. When Woody backed the car down the driveway to the street, the bump made Angie thrust her feet to the floorboards and groan. "Go easy, can't you?"

His heart pounding with anxiety, Woody sped toward the hospital only to have Angie cry out, "Slow down! This one's bad!"

And so it went: fast-slow-fast-slow…

Walking to the entrance, Angie had another big contraction and clung to Woody's neck until it passed. Inside, a very businesslike nurse took charge and deposited Angie in a wheelchair. "You wait here," she commanded Woody. Halfway down the hall, Angie turned and waved at him. Feeling worthless, he gave a half-hearted grin and waved back; then she disappeared around a corner. At loose ends, Woody bought a Coke from a vending machine and sat in the waiting room.

The wall clock read seven-ten. Woody picked up a copy of Vogue magazine, the only one on the table, and thumbed through it. The pages were filled with skinny women with scowls on their faces wearing silly looking dresses.

Seven-sixteen.

With a contemptuous toss, he chucked the publication aside. *I wonder if they have a Scientific American or Popular Mechanics somewhere.* He wandered around the room checking out the magazines. No luck.

Seven-nineteen.

A couple with a small boy holding a bandaged forearm came in and hurried to the desk. With worried looks, the parents murmured to the nurse, and soon an orderly whisked the whimpering boy down the same hall Angie had used. "He'll be fine," consoled the nurse behind the desk. The parents followed behind with worried faces.

Seven twenty-three.

Woody slouched in his chair and crossed his ankles. He thought he heard muffled screams from down the hall, but couldn't be certain whether it was Angie or the kid. He'd read in the 'How to Have Babies' books that emphasized labor could take hours, particularly with the first, so Woody sighed and looked at the clock.

Seven twenty-eight.

* * *

He woke with a start. The room dwelt in semi-darkness, illuminated only by dimmed overhead lights. An older man in a white coat stood in from of him, patting his forearm. "Mister Lawrence?"

Woody rubbed his cheeks. "Yeah."

"Congratulations are in order. You're the father of a healthy baby boy. Six pounds, fifteen ounces."

Woody's heart leapt. "Wow! And Angie? She okay?"

"She's fine. Tired, but nothing a little sleep wouldn't cure. We'll keep her for a day or two to make sure everything is all right. Give us a little time to square things away and you can go see her."

Woody glanced at the clock.

Two fifty-two.

With a bursting bladder, he raced to the restroom. *My water is about to break,* he joked to himself.

Three-ten

Woody stood impatiently staring down the hall, hands jammed in the pockets of his pants. His stomach rumbled with excitement. He wanted to see Angie, to hold her hand, to kiss her forehead. He wondered what the baby would look like. Did it have hair? A squarish face like his or a soft oval like Angie? Sleeping or fussing?

His musings abruptly ceased when a nurse came striding down the hall toward him. "I bet you're Mister Lawrence, right?" Her broad grin was genuine as if she shared the joy of the moment. "Come with me."

Relieved to be doing something other than waiting, Woody followed her brisk pace.

"The nursery is right around the corner. Let's visit your son first."

There, behind a large window, a dozen bassinets were set in two tidy rows. Only three held infants who were identified by large index cards.

The middle one said "Andros—Lawrence." Woody stared. His son had no hair and a red, wrinkled face. His arms and legs, bent as if to conserve space, reminded Woody of a crab. While the other two babies moved and thrashed about with jerky motions, his seemed comatose.

"Isn't he beautiful?" chimed the nurse.

Woody nodded automatically. "Let's go see Angie."

Piqued, Woody followed the nurse to her room where he found a radiant Angie—hair brushed back and fresh lipstick making her look like a joyous teen-ager. She patted the bed and smiled. "Sit."

Gingerly, he eased onto the bed and leaned over to kiss her lightly. "Feeling okay?"

"Let's just say I don't think I want to do this again. All the books say everyone thinks that, but soon forget that labor feels like crapping a damn hippo."

Woody took her hand. "Let's not worry about that now. The priority should be getting you back on your feet. To that end, I offer my humble services," he pronounced pontifically.

"Humble services? What's with this kind of talk?" She giggled. "Have you seen the baby? Isn't he gorgeous?"

"Yeah, saw him before I came in here. He's…" His voice trailed off.

"I hardly saw him in the delivery room and was kinda zonked out. He looked all wet and slippery—it's fantastic. He's our son—amazing."

The knots in Woody's shoulders vanished and he smiled. "You are incredible. How about another little kiss?"

* * *

The afternoon sun felt warm on the back of Woody's neck as he strolled in the park across the street from the hospital. Some of his misgivings had eased when he watched Angie breast-feed the baby. The two had blended into one—they fit together like first and second stages of a rocket. He sensed a mystery of the universe had unfolded before his eyes. He knew his world would never be the same again and he wondered about that.

If different, how? At first there would be midnight feedings, but Angie would take care of that. Off-the-cuff restaurant jaunts could get really complicated and volunteer work at the Yale orchestra would become hit-or-miss. The kid's wardrobe, not to mention diapers, promised to pressure their meager budget. Later on, potty training, and the terrible twos. Kindergarten, adolescence, and his first driver's license. College. Yale? His wedding—grandkids. Woody's mind staggered under fatherhood.

Then again, he could make matchstick rockets with the little guy. Explore the expanding world of space exploration. Share the crazy computer developments that were sure to come, like the new Macintosh just out. Become friends. Real friends.

What about his name? An ultrasound had showed it was a boy and Angie and Woody had constantly kicked around ideas, but couldn't pick a suitable one. He'd been embarrassed when the hospital staff asked about his name because it seemed tacky not to have one. He found a bench shaded from the August sun and sat down. His face screwed up in concentration as he sought a name for his son.

* * *

Now that visiting hours were over and Woody gone, glowing thoughts filled Angie's mind as she relaxed in the bed. She'd just nursed the baby, which slumbered in the crook of her arm. Motherhood cast a warm aura while a newfound sense of family settled over her.

Earlier that afternoon, her parents had come to visit and coo over their new grandson. Margaret, Angie's mother, swooned over the baby and declared he was the handsomest ever born, but expressed astonishment that the poor thing hadn't been named. Her husband George seemed indifferent about the matter saying, "A name is for life. Take your time."

The day nurse bustled in, her starched uniform rustling. "Job well done; I see. Let me have him so I can change the diaper and tuck him into his little bed. Give you a chance to relax or get some sleep."

"Thanks, but I have a lot on my mind; don't know if relaxation is in the cards, much less sleep."

With well-practiced motions, the nurse gathered the infant into her arms and left chatting to him in a sing-song voice, "We goin' to make you sparkling clean and happy."

Night had fallen and Angie gently rubbed her stomach to ease the cramps. The darkness crowded around and invited reflection on her new life. Obviously, her parents were thrilled and talked about spending more time together watching the tyke grow up. "I remember the first step you took," Margaret said.

"What can we do to help?" her father offered. "I can build a ramp down the front steps for the stroller." Mom insisted on helping with laundry and shopping. Angie sighed with pleasure. *That little guy is going to pull my family closer than ever.*

But what about Woody's father? She knew his parents were separated, maybe even divorced, but would Woody bother to tell his own father the good news? After all, they hadn't spoken for years. She surmised the chances that Woody would call his father were about the same as striking a golf ball all the way to Mars. *It's not fair.*

With deliberate motions, she reached for her small address book on the table next to her bed. *Woody might get pissed, but it's the right thing to do.* She picked up the phone and dialed, hoping the number was still good.

"Hello?"

"Mister Lawrence?"

"Speaking."

"You may not remember me; I'm Angie Andros, Woody's girlfriend."

"Woody? I don't know any Woody," he snarled.

Angie reeled at his harsh voice. She quickly took a deep breath and blurted, "You're a grandfather."

A prolonged silence was followed by, "What?"

"Woody and I have a day-old baby boy. That makes you a grandfather."

Nothing but silence.

"Mister Lawrence? Are you there?"

"Yeah." Another long pause. "Big surprise, huh?"

Angie could hear him coughing or gasping; she couldn't tell which. Suddenly, she realized he was crying. A few more moments passed and then he said, "Thanks for letting me know, Angie. I appreciate it. I'll sign off now."

Smiling, she slowly set the phone back in its cradle. *I better not tell Woody about this – he'll get mad for sure.*

The next morning a hospital attendant took Angie to the car in a wheelchair while a jittery Woody walked alongside. Ceremonially, they helped her into the passenger seat, handed her the infant, and were dispatched by the attendant with, "Good luck; the best to you."

Halfway home Angie said, "Woody, you can drive faster than twenty, you know. The baby isn't going to break."

"I'm just trying to make the trip comfortable for you."

She reached over and patted Woody's arm. Laughing, she said, "You're a sweet thing, but I'd be much more comfortable in my easy chair at home."

Woody pressed the accelerator and the car rocketed to twenty-five miles an hour.

* * *

The evening was soft and quiet as they settled into their chairs and chatted. The baby had been fed and slept soundly in the new crib. Woody leaned back and clasped his hands behind his head. "We have to decide on a name tonight. I can't imagine the most revolutionary scientist-to-be going nameless any more. You go first."

"Okay, what about my father's name—George?"

Woody grimaced inside. *Terrible name. Gotta be cool.* "That's a good one, but how about Harold?"

"Harold? You're nuts. That sounds like a goddamn name from the eighteenth century. I like John."

"As in John Wayne?" Woody grumbled. "No way. Why not Vincent?"

"You're kidding! Like Vincent Price?" Angie scowled in thought. "My uncle is named Samuel. That's not bad."

"That's no name for a guy who's going to set the world on fire. We need a prophetic name, one that will inspire him to greatness. Like Albert or Isaac."

"Like Einstein or Newton? You're being silly."

"Shawn."

"Phillip."

"Martin."

"Jason."

The doorbell interrupted their increasing frustration. Woody jumped to his feet. "I'll get it."

Wondering who'd be coming at the late hour, he opened the door and gasped. There stood his father. "May I come in?" he asked with a sheepish grin on his face.

Too stunned to speak, Woody simply stood aside.

Woodrow Junior walked in and looked at Angie, flushed with happiness seeing him.

Looking uncomfortable, he said to Angie, "Congratulations are in order. I trust all is well with you and the baby."

"Yes, thank you. We're both fine." She glanced at Woody and back to Woodrow, smiling. "Mister Lawrence, it appears that your son is in a state of shock."

"He's not the only one. This grandfather business is a jolt to my self-image of perpetual youth." He turned to his son. "I came, hat in hand, to see my grandson. Would that be all right?"

Still at a loss for words, Woody just nodded.

"Don't just stand there Woody; go get the friggin' baby," Angie commanded.

With a grunt, he walked to the back bedroom and picked up the sleeping infant. By the time he'd returned, the baby was fussing and squirming. Still feeling strange about his father and wondering how he knew, he moved to hand the infant to Angie.

"Mr. Lawrence, would you like to hold him?" Angie asked.

"Please call me Woodrow. And yes, I'd like that very much."

Awkwardly, Woody handed the baby to his father. "Be sure to support his head like I am," he cautioned.

Gingerly, Woodrow took the baby and sat down. "He's so tiny. I'd forgotten how small newborns are." Beaming, he looked up at Angie. "Look at his little fingers. Maybe someday they'll sign important legislation into law."

While Woody glowered, Angie smiled. "Or play a concert piano. One never knows."

Woodrow pulled a handkerchief from his pocket and mopped the drool from his coat sleeve. The kid began to bawl and kick. "I think he wants his mother." He stood and handed the baby to Angie. With a sigh, he said, "Well, I won't impose on you anymore. I'll take my leave." He moved toward the door and turned. "Thanks for letting me see my grandson. By the way, what's his name?"

Looking somewhat shamefaced, Angie said, "Just before you came, we were discussing that very thing. So far, we haven't decided."

Finding the courage to say something at last, Woody added, "We promised each other that by the end of the day, we'd have a name." He held the eyes of his father. "If you want, I could call you later tonight and tell you what we've decided."

Woodrow tilted his head. "That would be nice, Woodrow, er Woody." He stepped out the door and closed it softly behind him.

Woody looked at Angie, dumbfounded.

"I never would have guessed he'd do that," he muttered. "Father actually tried to be nice. Even called me Woody." He scratched his head. "I wonder how he found out about the baby?"

Blushing, Angie said, "I called him. After my folks came to the hospital and blubbered all over the place about their grandson, I figured it was only fair that your father knew too."

Grinning, Woody said, "It sure worked out, didn't it? I wonder how much we are going to see of him. Oh, well. Let's get back to the name problem."

Their faces twisted in concentration. "I'm stumped," Woody complained. "When I was five or six, I remember talking with my grandfather,

Woodrow Senior. I don't remember much except he smelled like pipe tobacco and talked really softly. I asked why the three of us had the same name. I told him I wanted my own name, not his or my father's. He told me it was because he was proud of his family and how pleased he felt when my father decided to continue the tradition."

Angie gently rocked the baby and straightened his gown. Suddenly she looked up and said, "There's only one name we can go with."

"What's that?"

"Woodrow Sterling Lawrence the Fourth."

"But my father is such a jerk!"

"Name our son after your grandfather." Angie snickered. "Or yourself. You're not a jerk—most of the time."

Late that night, Woody sipped a bit of champagne. "When I phoned, father seemed really pleased with our baby's name. What a day!"

Angie raised her glass in a toast. "Here's to our future, Woody, it's going to be super."

"There are two things on my mind right now," Woody pronounced. "First, what are we going to call our son? We need a nickname. Woody? With two Woody's in the same household, it will confuse everybody. The Fourth? That's stupid." His lips puckered in bewilderment.

Angie's face lit up. "Going back to those English classes of old, I remember drills with a thesaurus. One of the synonyms for four was quad. Let's call him Quad."

"Now *that's* weird! Quad—then again it does have a scientific ring to it. Not bad. But school kids will tease the daylights out of him." Woody abruptly grinned and slapped his thigh. "You're a genius, my love! Quad—our son's nickname!"

"There, that's settled. You said there were two things on your mind. What's the other?"

A serious look spread across Woody's face. "How can I say this? We've never mentioned it, but Quad is illegitimate. A bastard. That won't do if he's to become the greatest scientist in the universe—or maybe the greatest music composer."

"What are you saying?"

Woody set his glass down and knelt in front of Angie. "Will you marry me?"

* * *

George and Margaret, Angie's parents, had mixed feelings when their daughter announced that she planned to marry Woody as soon as possible. "Well, little wonder," Woody said to Angie, "I have a nothing job with piddly pay and no prospects. You're the one with a good career. I'll bet they're thinking that you're marrying beneath your potential."

"Don't be silly. They just don't know you. Wait until you dazzle them with that incredible imagination of yours. You'll find that 'foundation for big things' you always talked about. You'll make it happen; I know."

"I hate to tell you, but my normal inspirations haven't been coming lately. My job smothers my brain; it's only data entry for crying out loud! A grade school kid can do that." Then his face lit up. "On the flip side, I have other things on my mind; Quad for instance. I'm thinking he could be that foundation. Might be almost as important as our wedding!" He rubbed his chin. "Speaking of that, I have no idea on how to plan an event like that. Guess we have to get a license, huh?"

"That's the scientist in you talking. Forget the mechanics for now. What kind of wedding do you want? Formal with tuxes and a fancy gown? Hundreds of guests?"

"No way," Woody scowled. "Unless you want to," he corrected.

"My parents are high-flying business people and yours is a powerful lawyer. They'd probably like a formal one, but you and I are really easy-going people. You know, casual."

"Besides, big weddings are super-expensive."

"I'm sure my parents would foot the bill," Angie countered. "It's the responsibility of the bride's family anyway." She tugged her earlobe in thought. "You know, I heard there are small wedding chapels that take care of everything. We could think about that. Or maybe in a church?"

"Chapels? Like Las Vegas?"

"No, that's too glitzy. I'm not sure, but there may be one or two right here in town."

Woody grimaced. "This is getting complicated. Gotta find a place to get married, pick someone to conduct the ceremony, get a best man and maid of honor, flowers..."

"There you go, bogging down in mechanics again." Angie wagged her finger at Woody. "Let's stay on track—what kind of wedding?"

"Okay, okay. Not formal. How about something simple? Maybe a chapel is a good idea. Do they have a menu of ceremonies we can choose from?"

Angie laughed. "There you go again. How would I know? I've never been married before. You said simple. How simple? If you want really, really simple, we could even get married on the beach."

Woody waved his hand, "Naw, that's...we can?" he blurted.

"Sure. People do it all the time."

"Really?" Woody slapped his thigh. "Let's get married on the beach!"

"At sunset. That would be *so* romantic."

Relieved the issue was resolved, Woody set his record of Beethoven's Ninth on the turntable, turned it on, and they cuddled together in bliss.

* * *

"I'll take care of all the arrangements," Angie said the next morning at breakfast. "All you have to do is show up, okay?"

Pleased to be relieved of a tedious endeavor for which he had no knowledge, Woody nodded happily. "That's fine with me." He pushed aside a vague sense of guilt and repeated, "Just fine."

Angie met with a Gateway official who handled travel arrangements for the school. "A beach wedding?" He said. "There's only one place for that, the Lighthouse Point Park. My daughter got hitched there."

Armed with that, Angie searched through the yellow pages that afternoon and found several nearby wedding chapels. "This is what we want," she told them. "A person to conduct the ceremony, a civil one with a justice of the peace or someone like that. We'll write our own vows. Plan for maybe fifty guests at most, so we'll need chairs. Here's the hitch, I want the wedding to take place at Lighthouse Point Park. On the sand—just before sundown. I've heard there's a small pavilion for refreshments. Nothing fancy. Can you do that?"

Within two days she selected Mountain Laurel Wedding Chapel to coordinate things. It specialized in outdoor ceremonies and had managed several at the Lighthouse Point Park. "They have a very nice carousel," they advised, "but it closes at sundown. You may want to plan some festivities before the actual wedding. Do you have a date in mind?"

"This Saturday?"

A chuckle, "Oh dear, we're booked three weeks out. Besides, we'll need time to pull everything together. If you can get by with a delay, let's meet and discuss everything."

With a sigh of exasperation about putting off the wedding, Angie took Woody to the chapel the next day after work. It took over two hours to settle all the details: flowers, champagne, officiant, an ornate trellis to stand under, glassware, and invitations. Afterwards, they went to the Vital Records Office and got their marriage license.

Following her last class the next afternoon, Angie connected with Maureen, her older sister, and asked if she'd be Maid of Honor. With a whoop, she accepted. The rest of the day was filled with giggles and hilarity as they met to address invitations Angie had purchased that morning. After consulting their mother, they came up with only twenty-six guests. "Tonight, I'll check with Woody to see who he wants to invite," Angie said.

That night Woody came home exhausted, not from working, but from boredom. He grabbed a Coke from the refrigerator and collapsed in his chair. "How did school go today, Angie?"

"Forget school; I've been working on invitations. I've taken care of my side of the family, but we need to talk about who you and your father want to come."

"Odd you say that. I've been totally preoccupied with our wedding all day. So much, I made half a dozen input errors. Caught hell from the boss.

"Back to your question, I don't have any friends except Jose and Peggy from high school. I could invite them, I suppose. Then there's Randy, but he's in Atlanta. Thinkin' I'll give him a call and ask if he'd be my best man. Other than that, it's up to my father."

"Well, don't just sit there; call Randy and your dad." She handed him the phone.

Two days later the guest list had been completed: Randy joyously accepted Woody's invitation to be Best Man saying he'd fly into Boston's Logan International the day before. Woody's father, plus Jose and Peggy, rounded out Angie's list.

"Looks like the groom's side of the aisle will be a little thin," Angie grumbled.

"We going to draw lines in the sand to define an aisle?" Woody retorted. "Just a few folding chairs scattered on the beach, right?"

Angie rolled her eyes to the ceiling in disgust, drew a deep breath, and tried to sort through her thoughts. But a howl from Quad sent her scurrying down the hall.

Later, Angie burped the baby and then jiggled him on her knee. She gazed at Woody with an apologetic look on her face. "Considering you went from disowned to an awkward relationship with your father, we're lucky to have him come to our wedding." She leaned over and kissed Quad's bald head. "Having a baby is like a big magnet. It draws people together, especially grandparents."

Woody grinned. "I may still be disowned. Father hasn't mentioned it."

Later that night, their heads hovered over the computer keyboard as they haggled over the wedding vows. "Today we commit the rest or our lives…"

The early morning hours found the couple entwined in slumber while the computer monitor glowed with satisfaction in the living room.

* * *

Wedding day! The small crew from the chapel trundled through the sand, setting chairs in place and positioning pots of yellow roses, sunflowers, and fiery lilies along a path to the ceremonial arch.

A table in the small pavilion glistened with sparkling glassware, champagne bottles, and plates of hors d'oeuvres. In its center, a wedding cake was crowned with a figure of a bride and groom standing proudly arm in arm.

As if it understood the import of the occasion, the sun hovered low over Long Island Sound and the beaches of West Haven, shooting crimson rays over the gathering guests. Laughter burst from the nearby carousel where, on the sly, Woodrow Junior had paid everyone's admission for the half-hour before it closed for the night.

In separate accommodations adjacent to the carousel, Woody and Angie dressed in casual outfits with the help of Maureen and Randy. Casting aside stuffy tradition, they mounted adjoining horses on the carousel, yelling and screaming in delight. Maureen clambered onto the carousel and sat on a fancy bench right behind the boisterous wedding couple with a wide-eyed Quad riding in her arms.

As the sun was about to touch the horizon, they dismounted and walked toward the ornate arch at water's edge to be married. Suddenly,

Woody stopped and gently took Angie in his arms. Tears blurring his vision, he said, "This moment is the beginning of my life as a husband as well as a father. You and Quad bring a new world to me, one that will override my old erratic ways and set me on the road to fulfill our dreams. Your dreams will become our dreams. I love you." He coughed to clear his throat, pleased his little speech brought a tear to Angie's eyes as well as his own.

Ignoring tradition once more, Woody put his arm around Angie's waist and led her between the potted flowers to be wed. On one side Woody saw Jose and Peggy, both with wide smiles—pumping their fists. Woody's father sat in the first row looking serious while Angie's parents watched, wearing tight grins. Randy and Maureen stood stiffly alongside the arch as Quad rested quietly in Maureen's arms.

Still clutching one another, Woody and Angie approached the officiant with solemn strides. Maureen stepped over and handed Quad to Angie. The baby quietly settled in the crook of her arm and grinned.

"We are gathered here to celebrate..."

A wave hissed up onto the sandy slope, but Woody didn't notice. The guests pressed closer to hear the words, but Woody didn't notice. His eyes were only for Angie and Quad. When the moment came to recite their vows, the sun touched the distant horizon while brilliant red hues lanced onto the scattered clouds. Carefully, he joined Angie in holding the baby and they began reciting their vows. "Today we commit the rest of our lives..." Woody realized these words were sacred, to direct his entire future. Toward the end, Angie spoke, "I pledge to you my undying love."

Woody replied, "And I pledge to you my undying love."

Everyone laughed when the words, "You may kiss the bride," was thwarted by a baby boy squirming between the newlyweds.

Woodrow Junior sprang from his chair and turned to Angie. "I've always wanted a daughter and now it's happened. Welcome to the family." He nodded at Quad. "If I may, with Maureen's help, I'll mind the little heir apparent. I'm sure you two will want to circulate."

The caterers popped champagne corks and filled chilled flutes while managing a surge of guests pressing through the sand to the pavilion. In a daze, Woody stood alongside Angie. *First, I became a father and now I'm a husband.* He turned and gazed at Angie's face, made pink by the fading sunset. *This must be heaven.*

* * *

Because their jobs and finances squashed any chance of a real honeymoon, they returned to their apartment where they nibbled on wedding cake and sipped champagne snitched from the beach. Woody, as was his tradition, presented Angie with a tiny stuffed kitty with enormous eyes, drawing giggles from his bride. Later, their modest festivities were dampened by Quad's fussing which called Angie from their wedding bed.

Half an hour later, Angie returned with Quad in her arms. Shaking his head, Woody grumbled, "You deserve a real honeymoon, my love. You shouldn't be spending our big day in a grubby apartment."

"We agreed to celebrate together however the stars allow. I can't get away from my teaching in mid-term and all of our money put together wouldn't buy bus fare to downtown Boston."

"I know. I just want to be the best husband ever."

Angie held Quad up to Woody. "Look, you already are!"

* * *

As married couples do, they soon settled into a routine: Woody dragging himself to a tedious job while Angie continued to refine her lesson plans. Quad, work schedules, and housekeeping chores allowing, both spent as much time as they could volunteering at the Yale Symphony Orchestra. Maureen, being a bookkeeper working from home, graciously volunteered to babysit Quad whenever her appointments allowed. From time to time, other babysitters recommended by friends filled in.

"I have to find another job," Woody complained one day. "A monkey would be bored out of his mind." He waved three letters at Angie. "More résumés going out, but nobody is interested in a college dropout with no significant work experience."

"I know you hate working there, but every dime helps."

"It feels really dumb that you make more money than I do. I'm supposed to be the breadwinner."

"I feel a change in the wind, Woody. My pay isn't all *that* much, but insurance is great. If I teach thirty years, I'll get a good pension, but if I'm honest, my job is becoming tiresome."

"Really?"

"My first year was exciting, but now that I've worked up all the lesson plans, one semester is like the next. I find myself looking forward to volunteering at the orchestra where they keep changing the productions. Keeps me on my toes."

Woody draped his arm over her shoulder and smiled. "You know, I'm the same way. I'm learning a lot about staging and music. Which reminds me, we're due at the music hall in an hour."

The Herald American
Thursday, January 3, 1985
Section D1: Entertainment

Leontyne Price Retires

Her Last Performance will be Aida at the Met

Hearing the news about Leontyne Price, Angie went on an opera kick, listening to as many of her recordings as she could find. Slowly, Woody started appreciating the soprano and opera in general, but they didn't displace Beethoven as Woody's favorite.

Things slowed a week after the New Year. A heavy snow smothered their neighborhood in silence, so they bundled Quad in blankets, booties and a cap for a stroll, embracing the winter calm. Looking back at the holiday season, Woody hated everything about it. The exploding number of retail transactions with Baker Financial swamped him and on top of that, Yale decided to produce the Nutcracker ballet during the weeks before Christmas. Because the dancers commanded the stage, the orchestra had to be moved to the pit, a complicated process. Electrical power and lighting requirements doubled and then management had decided to record the performances—two matinees and four evening productions. In a daze, Woody fought complicated electronic setups, getting only three or four hours sleep a night.

In a like manner, Angie had been pressed into service at the Community College supporting holiday events: a parade featuring the school band, caroling by the show choir, and a holiday concert by the orchestra. She too, became bone-tired and the newlyweds rarely saw one another. Maureen, Angie's sister, began complaining about all the hours she spent babysitting Quad. Other possible sitters voiced reluctance to abandon their holiday celebrations, yet the new parents somehow managed. The night of New Year's Eve found them both asleep by nine. Quad was inconsiderate and fussed most of the evening.

Things became even worse when Woody returned to work. His desk had been inundated with paperwork that his boss piled up during the time the office was closed between Christmas and New Year's Day. Then he scheduled heavy overtime for Woody trying to recover. Conversely, Angie had been greeted by mellow co-workers and students sporting new Christmas sweaters and relaxed grins. Unlike her husband, she looked forward to the next few weeks, which promised to be a relaxing pause after the hectic pace of the holidays.

But concern crossed her mind when Dean Rasmussen summoned her to his office. "Sit," he commanded. "Cup of coffee?"

"Yes, that would be nice."

He poured from a carafe on his desk. "Sugar? Creamer?"

"No thanks."

"Well, Mrs. Lawrence, I have a problem."

Nervous, Angie bit her lip. "What's that?"

"Mr. Teague, our music director, has developed pretty serious arthritis over the years and has decided to resign from the staff. I'm not surprised, truth-be-known. He's sixty-eight."

"That's too bad. I work very well with him. He'll be missed."

The Dean fixed her with a steady gaze. "You haven't been with Gateway College very long, have you? Two? Two-and-a-half years?"

Angie nodded.

"Even so, I'm very impressed with the work you've been doing, particularly over the holiday crunch. To use a common expression, you saved our bacon. So, rather than start an outside search for Teague's replacement, I'd like to offer you the position." He quizzically raised his eyebrow.

"Me? Music director?" Angie gasped.

"Why not? There's a lot to the job, I know—overseeing the orchestra, band, and the choir. I realize that's all very intimidating, so I've asked Teague to stay until the end of the term so he can bring you along in an orderly fashion."

"I'm stunned."

"There will be a nice pay increase, of course. What do you say?"

"Can I continue to teach my music appreciation class? The kids are great."

"Certainly."

"Count me in!"

* * *

Woody had mixed feelings about Angie's promotion when she brought the news home. "Wow!" he exclaimed. "We never saw that in the cards. Big raise, too," he pouted, reflecting on his own job situation. "Seems like you're wearing the pants in the family. I'm stuck in a stupid job making half the money you are. You must be disappointed in me."

"Get off that crap!" Angie shouted. "Are you going to sit around and mope, or are you going to do something? Want to know how I became music director? Rasmussen told me it's because I stepped up to the Christmas madness. I saved their bacon, he said. Went the extra mile, all that stuff. Sound familiar?"

Woody cringed at her onslaught. "What do you mean?"

"How did you spend the last couple of months? Sitting on your butt?"

"You know I didn't. Worked twenty hours a day."

"Well?"

"Where are you going with this? Nobody but Baker Finance and Yale even know I'm alive."

"Well?"

Outdone with Angie's cryptic comments, Woody threw up his hands and exclaimed, "I'm going to take a walk." He yanked on his heavy jacket and stomped out.

Woody jammed his bare hands into the coat pockets and shivered as the wind whipped up snowflakes that sparkled in the bright winter sun. *Why am I mad at Angie? I'm the jerk.* His mind whirled as he tried to sort out why Angie kept asking "Well?"

Okay, she got promoted at her school because she "saved their bacon." Why would I want to get promoted at Baker? It's an incredibly stupid place with no future. Then he thought of Yale. *That's not even a job; I work for free.* He kicked a clump of snow. *Just thinking about it, I saved their bacon, too.* Abruptly, a wide smile spread across his face, and he spun and walked briskly back to the apartment—his eyelids twitching.

"Angie, I have an idea!" he yelled striding into the apartment. He found her in the kitchen rinsing dishes. He grabbed her shoulders, turned her around, and gave her a big hug, ignoring her dripping hands. "My thoughts may be pie-in-the-sky, but it's something."

Still irked by his abrupt exit, she said in a frosty tone, "Well?"

Woody laughed. "There you go with the *Well* again. It's a very deep subject, you know."

"I hope your idea is better than that ancient play on words."

"I'll let you decide. Come on; let's go sit down in the living room."

They plopped on the sofa and Woody pivoted to face Angie directly. "The key words here are 'saved their bacon.' You got promoted because you saved Gateway's bacon. Your exact words."

"Yes. I remember."

"Well…" Woody caught himself saying the *W* word. "I was about to say that I don't give a hoot about Baker Finance, but Yale is something else. In a very real sense, I saved their bacon, too. I've never really worked for them, just volunteered, but what if I tried to get them to hire me?"

"Well, where did you think I was going with all those wells?" Angie smirked.

"You devil! You devious little devil!"

She giggled and took Woody's hands. "Now that you've discovered my true nature, tell me how you're going to convince Yale to bring you on."

Playfully, he began, "*Well,* I haven't figured that part out yet."

"Okay, Mr. Scientific Man, they can't hire you unless they need you. There has to be an opening of some sort. What were you doing all that time you were saving their bacon?"

"I set up electrical outlets in the pit and installed a bunch of new lights. Put gels on them, worked on the cameras they wanted, set up microphones, wrote schedules for the lighting, did all the computer work…"

"Enough! Enough! Question: who helped you? Who else could do the job?"

Puzzled, Woody asked, "What do you mean? I did it all by myself, except for one or two freshman kids who are supposed to help me. They're just gofers. Only did what I told them."

"What do you do in normal times, when it's not the holidays?"

"It's not much different. They leave all that electrical and computer stuff to me. Everyone else has been given other special assignments." He rubbed his chin. "Thinking back, it wasn't like that when I first started volunteering. I think they transferred their regular electrician to a new position—campus-wide maintenance or something. I haven't seen him in a long while. Plus, I'm the only person who can make the computer sing."

"Well?"

Woody squeezed Angie's hands. "I guess they need a good electrician and maybe a computer guy too."

"That sounds like an opening in the organization that Yale needs to fill—particularly if a certain devoted volunteer decides to cut back—if you know what I'm saying," she said with a wink.

Quad's fussing in the back bedroom brought the discussion to a halt. As Angie walked down the hall to his aid, Woody called out, "You *are* a devious devil!" He vowed to get her a nice bouquet of flowers from the supermarket. She already had too many fuzzy stuffed kittens, which presently resided in Quad's playpen.

* * *

Woody switched off the house lights in the auditorium and sucked in a deep breath to calm his nerves. After a week of rehearsing interview tactics with Angie, the time had come to approach Sam, the house manager, for a real job. As night fell, the usual sounds of chaos faded and Woody figured that Sam would be in his office tidying up the last of the day's details.

As expected, the door was open, and Woody stepped in. "Got a minute?"

"Sure. Have a seat. What's on your mind?"

"Well..." (*There's that word again.*) "I'm not sure how to go about this." *(Angie said to sound humble.)* "There's a problem at my work. They want me to put in a lot of extra hours; they're really busy." (*White lie, now that the holidays were over and he'd caught up on the mess.*) "I'm not sure how much time I'll be able to spend here with the orchestra."

Sam scowled. "That could make things tough around here, Woody. We've come to rely on you. Can you work out something at your job so you're not needed so much?"

"No. I've already asked. Besides I can use the overtime pay. I'll really miss working here with everyone and I'm hooked on the music too. No matter, I guess. I have a couple of Beethoven records at home." *(He'd developed the script with Angie.)*

"I wish we could adjust your hours here at Yale, but we're driven by performance schedules. Are you stuck with the hours you work at…?"

"Baker Finance. Afraid so. I wish things were different so I could volunteer here all the time. But I have a new wife, a new baby…"

Sam laced his fingers and put them behind his head. His eyes raked the ceiling.

Woody felt jittery in the silence. (*Be patient, Angie said. Don't look nervous.)* He looked at the wall behind Sam, afraid to engage the man eye to eye. Among numerous awards, there was a diploma proclaiming Sam's doctorate degree. The man's status made Woody even more fidgety.

"What do you do at this Baker place? Finance you said?"

"I work with computers," Woody explained. "Billing, accounts receivable, that sort of thing."

"Computers? That's interesting because I'd be hard pressed to justify hiring an electrician type—you're not even licensed. But computers are a different thing. You also do all the computer stuff, right? Tell me more."

A spark of hope flashed in Woody's mind. Skipping Baker altogether, he talked about spreadsheets, his work combining music with computers (not mentioning the Korg concert part), and his program that boosted sales at the music store. His excitement carried him away and he finished breathless.

Sam seemed mesmerized. "Young man, that's impressive. But I can't afford to hire a full-time computer expert either. We're just a small organization."

Gloom settled over Woody. "Isn't there some way to come up with a job description that combines computer work, electrical, and stage management? Kinda what I've been doing all along. I know you need help with all that." *(Don't beg, Angie said).*

Sam's eyebrows narrowed in thought. "It is obvious you are qualified, even for the electrical work you've been doing," he acknowledged. "You're an ace on the computer and together they might make a full-time position. You'd be willing to take all that on?"

Stunned, all Woody could do was bob his head.

"All right, here's what I can do." Sam leaned back in his chair and crossed his arms. "You've been dynamite help around here so your work ethic isn't in doubt. With a little luck, we might make a deal. But I can't authorize a new-hire without blessings from the powers that be. The bean counters, you know. Give me a day or two and I'll get back to you, okay?"

"That's great!" *(Always stay calm, Angie had admonished.)* "I don't know how to thank you!"

* * *

Miraculously, Woody didn't get a speeding ticket as he raced home to tell Angie. He vaulted up the porch steps and burst through the door. "Angie! Where are you?" Then he remembered she was probably picking up Quad at her sister's place, a short walk away. The news would have to wait. After grabbing a Coke from the fridge, Woody plopped in his chair. A replay of the meeting with Sam danced in his mind and the realization that he assumed the "powers that be" would approve his job might be optimistic. With a wave of his hand, Woody pushed any doubt aside.

It wasn't long before Angie struggled through the door, Quad in one arm while pulling the stroller inside with the other.

Woody leapt from the chair yelling, "Angie, I got the job!"

"That's wonderful!" she cried out. "Let me put Quad to bed and you can fill me in."

Thankfully Quad fell asleep before his head hit the mattress. "Alright, Mister Go-Getter, tell me the deal," Angie said, briskly coming up the hall. "This is exciting!"

His chest puffed out in pride, Woody explained the meeting with Sam in detail.

"I'm confused, Woody. When do you start?"

Looking a little sheepish, he said, "A few things need to be sorted out before I report to work."

"For instance?"

"Sam has to get approval from administration before he can hire anyone. But there's no doubt in my mind it's a go."

"You certain?"

"You bet."

"What will your salary be?"

A blush crept over Woody's face. "We didn't get around to talking about that, but anything is better than Baker Finance."

Angie became frustrated. "What else is up in the air?"

Woody swallowed hard. "Didn't get around to talking about the hours or insurance or vacation. But we'll work all that out—you'll see. Sam's gonna call in a day or two, then we can go over all those details. I'm totally pumped up! I'll be doing something that really matters to me, Angie. I can't wait to jump in! I even get to listen to all that music for free! You know how I've become about music."

His enthusiasm and beaming face swept away Angie's irritation about all the details, as he called them. She knew Sam and had faith in her husband. With a bit of luck, all would turn out fine. She rose, gave Woody an immense hug and went to open a bottle of wine.

* * *

Hunched over his computer at Baker Finance, Woody conjured scenarios of how he'd tell the boss to take the job and stuff it up his left nostril. Maybe he'd brag: *"I've landed this phenomenal job doing exotic computer work for Yale."* Then again, he thought: *"You know, you've never considered any of my suggestions to make things run better, so…"* Maybe just a simple, *"I quit this lousy job."* At lunchtime, he telephoned Yale to see if Sam had any news yet. He hadn't felt this frisky in months.

Sam was away on an errand and didn't leave a message, so Woody went back to Baker figuring to check with Sam again that night.

Before he left for home that night, Woody called once more and Sam, sounding somewhat annoyed, said, "They're thinking about it. No decision yet."

Mildly disappointed, he drove to the apartment and greeted Angie and Quad with laughter and smiles, pretending the lack of good news didn't bother him. "I'll hear from Sam tomorrow for sure, Angie. He said no more than two days."

In fact, a full week passed with no word. All Sam could say is, "You know bureaucracy; they make a sloth look like a racehorse." His words of comfort did little to mollify Woody's anxiety.

Saturday afternoon at Yale, Woody perched on a ladder adjusting the overhead lights for the night's piano soloist when Sam yelled up at him.

"Got the go-ahead! Come on down; we need to talk."

Euphoric, Woody hit the floor in an instant and hustled to Sam's office. "They had trouble figuring out how a stagehand could be a computer guru, too," Sam smiled. "I had to write up a justification for them. Took time."

Woody pumped Sam's hand. "Thank you, thank you!"

"We need to talk about your pay. We can't offer much at first, but we can take another look at your ninety-day review."

Woody didn't care what they paid as long as it was more than Angie made. That would assuage his male ego. "I'm ready."

"How does $425 a week sound?"

"Oh. Well," he gulped. "That sounds okay I guess." *Punt. Angie makes $680 a week. But at least $425 is a bunch more than Baker pays.* "You said I might get a raise after ninety days?"

"Yeah, that's standard. A lot would depend on how well you do on the computer. We'll need your thoughts on how to upgrade our capability;

the big boss wants big things in data management. We've taken your word about your skills in that department. We did check out that A—Sharp music store. Sounds like sales were on a roll before they were bought out."

"Sure were," he bubbled. "I planned to take my sales program across the whole organization, and…oh never mind. The sale killed that idea."

"Fine, the pay issue is settled. Our insurance isn't much; has a big deductible. Let me show you the particulars."

"Don't bother. My wife Angie has good coverage through Gateway City College. I'm sure the two policies together will take care of our needs."

"That's right; you're married to Angie. You're a lucky man."

Twenty minutes later they'd settled on sick leave, vacation time and the start date. Woody raced out of the office for his car. *Angie will be thrilled. A real job. With Yale no less!*

* * *

A wave of contentment swept over Angie. Finally, Woody's ongoing tirades against Baker Finance would cease. Her skepticism that his job at the orchestra, another of Woody's typical pipedreams, vanished, replaced by newfound confidence in her husband. Gone was the lurking worry that the burden of a semi-functional spouse coupled with Quad's upbringing would fester as the months passed. Her faith in Woody's vivid imagination and ability to innovate blossomed once more and the duo of her husband and Sam working side-by-side smacked of a Rodgers and Hammerstein success story. She cuddled up to Woody and sipped a taste of wine. "Thanks for the flowers; they're beautiful." She patted his leg. "Are you going to give notice at Baker in the morning?"

"Sure! Two weeks is usual, but I really want to give the boss a piece of my mind, pack up my stuff, and leave on the spot."

"Not cool," she admonished. "Be professional. Yale can wait a couple of weeks." She reached over to the playpen and tickled Quad with a stuffed kitten as he gurgled in pleasure. *Even our little guy seems to know there's been a big change in our family's fortune.*

Early the next morning Woody strode into Baker Financial and confronted his boss. "Hank, I'm quitting; giving two weeks' notice."

"Just like that, huh? I've been thinking about canning your ass anyway. You've been working half-speed and plodding around like a zombie."

"Well, in two weeks you'll be rid of me."

Hank scowled. "You know, I don't need two more weeks of your screwing up. It's a good thing that data entry guys are dime a dozen. I can have you replaced just like that." He snapped his fingers. "Let's clear out your desk right now."

"Suits me!"

Elated, he drove to the apartment only to find it empty because Angie was at school while Maureen babysat Quad. He picked up the phone and dialed Yale. "Sam, good news! I can start right away. Baker turned down my offer of two weeks' notice. I'm free!"

"You busy today?"

"Nope."

"Come on by late this afternoon. We'll fill out all the paperwork and pass the good news."

Unsure how long he'd be away, Woody jotted a note for Angie and drove to the concert hall. There, Sam led him to the human resources office where a pile of forms awaited his attention. Once that tedious task wrapped up, Sam ushered Woody to a battered desk in a dingy area near the lighting booth. "This is yours," Sam said. "It will have to do for now. We've never had a 'Special Stage Technician' before, so we don't have a good spot for you yet. It's the best I could do on such short notice."

Noticing a desktop computer perched on the desk Woody said, "This is perfect."

"I tried to clean your desk and rustle up paper, pens, a telephone directory, and other basics. You'll have to wait a day or two to get your phone hooked up. Let me know if you need anything else."

"No need to bother; I've been rattling around this place for ages. I know my way around." He pulled up the chair, slapped the desk, and said, "What's my first assignment?"

Sam grinned. "Hadn't figured you'd actually start work today. It's getting late, you know. Come back at eight in the morning and I'll get you started. There are a few hiccups in the radio broadcast equipment. It's all Greek to me, so maybe that's your first task."

"Right up my alley!"

That night, Woody invited his father over for dinner and basked in Woodrow's praise.

The Herald American
Friday, March 24, 1989

Massive Oil Spill in Alaska!

Exxon Valdez Runs Aground Spilling 11 Million Gallons of Crude

Nearly five years old, Quad had become a holy terror. Possessing the boundless energy of his age, he raced down the hall chasing Wernher von Braun, the cat. Howling, the animal bolted under the sofa where Woody sat reading the newspaper. "Quad, simmer down," Woody scolded. As the boy groped under the couch for the petrified cat, Woody calmly turned the page and continued reading about the Exxon Valdez oil spill. Giving up on the cat, Quad jumped alongside his father and pointed to a photo of the ship. "What's that?"

"It's a big ship that carries oil. It ran aground on a reef and spilled a bunch of oil into the ocean."

"What's a reef?"

Woody smiled and patted his son's head. *This kid. I can't decide if he's packed full of questions or wild mischief.* He called out to Angie, "Check out this story on a humongous oil spill up in Alaska. It's wild."

"Later. I have to finish paperwork for my students if they're to go to Yale's concert. Liability waivers and insurance. Dang lawyers drive me up the wall."

Woody chuckled. "I know what you're saying." He checked his watch. "I have to get going. Gotta trouble-shoot the new amplifier by ten this morning." He snatched his briefcase, pecked Angie on the cheek, and flew through the front door calling out, "Quad's after Wernher again. See to it, okay?"

Threading through traffic, he reflected on his recent promotion. *It certainly isn't like the old volunteering days. Now I'm doing all the computer work, handling production details as well as maintaining the broadcast and sound systems. Guess I'm flattered to be kicked up to "Assistant Manager". Not bad for a twenty-nine-year-old. Good thing that new computer is saving my butt.*

Nodding to the stagehands, he threaded his way to his desk, the old one by the lighting booth. He didn't care for his new one in the administration area surrounded by a bunch of suits. He smiled with pleasure as a soprano and a mezzo-soprano rehearsed the Flower Duet by Delibes. *What a piece! Almost brings tears to my eyes. Can't hear that in the fancy new office!*

Finally, the frantic day, filled with problems, wound down. Plans for the next concert had been resolved for the most part. He wondered how Angie was doing with her project to bring her students to tour the Yale facility and attend a performance that included Pachelbel's Canon in D, one of his favorites. She'd been working mostly with Sam, but he'd helped too. He kicked his feet up on the desk and breathed a happy sigh, remembering how Angie had grumped about teaching the same material year after year. Consequently, she decided to expand the school's offerings by taking her class to a big-time concert at Yale. A wistful feeling tugged at him. *I used to do that sort of thing – conjure wild ideas.*

Slowly, an idea turned over in his head. *Angie is bringing her music appreciation class, but what about science majors? History majors? Football players?* He knew that few students were into classical music, but what if he could show them the magnificent mystery of Beethoven? Maybe come up with an incentive? He jerked to his feet with a long-forgotten flutter in his eye. He found Sam in the stock room opening boxes of programs for the evening performance.

"Hi, Sam. Let me help." As Woody leaned over to gather up the pamphlets, he said, "Angie is bringing her class to see the Pachelbel concert. It's sure to be an eye-opener for them, right?"

"Yeah. It'll be a big step up from their small Gateway College orchestra. I mean, we're a big-time touring orchestra, and they have, what, thirty-five members? Ours is ninety."

"Is it a lot of trouble to handle a school group like that?"

"Naw. We do that sort of thing from time to time. Good for community relations."

"Suppose Angie and I make arrangements to bring in twenty students at a time. Maybe a group every month? Yale could promote the thing as proving that an elite university can reach out to regular kids and show them *real* music, not that crap they listen to."

Sam paused unpacking programs and looked over at Woody. "You know, I had a similar idea a couple of years ago, but couldn't figure out a way to do it. Maybe a tie-in with Gateway could make it happen."

"Is that something you could get going?"

Sam sat on a carton and smiled. "You work the Gateway end and I'll get approval from our front office. If we can make this happen, not only will New Haven rejoice, but maybe Yale can convince a bunch of hormone-driven adolescents to dig Mozart."

Woody sat on a box alongside Sam. "Most of them would rather take an advanced calculus class than sit through a symphony. I'm thinking we need to come up with some kind of incentive; call it a bribe."

A frown crossed Sam's face. "A bribe?"

"How about giving out Yale baseball caps to everyone who signs up? Even girls wear them these days."

Obviously relieved, Sam slapped his knee. "Good idea! If you work with Angie to line up Gateway, I'll take care of Yale."

Just Gateway? This is only the beginning. "I'll be in touch."

* * *

A chilly rain beat on Woody's face as he ran to the car. As he slipped inside, he twisted the key to start the old clunker he bought using his recent raise. Driving the nicer car, Angie and Quad could stay dry on days like this when she picked up the little guy at her sister's house. Traffic and red lights thwarted his eagerness to get home to his wife and start the ball rolling.

Finally, he burst through the front door yelling, "Angie!"

"Do you always have to make an entrance like Sherman's march through Georgia?"

"I have news! Big news! One of my inspirations hit me this afternoon. Just like the old days! Sit down and I'll reveal the magic."

Quad ran up and embraced Woody's knees. "Why don't you stay and hear my idea, little man?" He patted the sofa cushion between himself and Angie. "Park yourself right here."

He gave them both a squeeze and took a deep breath. "Angie, I bet your class is really excited about going to a Yale concert, huh?"

"They sure are. I've lectured on various composers, emphasizing Pachelbel of course. But now I'm also explaining all the features of a large orchestra. Why do you ask?"

A wide smile creased Woody's face. "How many kids are you thinking about taking if we get a go-ahead, just the twenty?"

"Actually, I'll bet I could get release slips for almost the entire class."

"Too bad we're limited to twenty—Sam's orders," Woody said. "Twenty is good, but would you get upset if a hundred signed up?"

"You're nuts. My class is only thirty."

"I believe there are around 1,500 students at Gateway, right?" Woody reached over Quad and patted Angie's hand. "Suppose you and I persuade the powers-that-be to pull together groups of twenty or thirty students every month? We could bring Bach and Beethoven to a bunch of people. Strauss waltzes too. What do you think?"

"I think you *are* nuts. You actually believe the Yale Orchestra would buy into another of your wild schemes?"

Woody leaned back and tickled Quad, who screamed with pleasure. "Not only do I believe they will, I *know* they will. Sam and I cut a deal this morning. All that remains is for the key member of Gateway's music department to clear it with the dean. That would be you, I believe."

Angie gasped. "He gave you the go-ahead? That's wonderful! My head is swimming! I shouldn't have any trouble getting Dean Rasmussen to go along; he's been very supportive in the past." She blushed. "I think he has a crush on me."

"I think every man alive has a crush on you, Angie." Woody flexed his meager bicep. "If he gets too fresh, I'll punch him out."

The next evening, Angie gleefully told Woody that Rasmussen loved the idea and asked her to coordinate everything. While swinging Quad in circles, she danced foot-to-foot in excitement. Woody uncorked a bottle of cheap cabernet and said, "We've got the ball, my love. Now we need a plan." Later that night, the old passion returned to their lovemaking, reminiscent of the *Angie's Raft* days.

That weekend, while Maureen took Quad to the zoo, Woody and Angie "knocked heads" about promotion, transportation, and irksome things like liability insurance. Angie dashed another note on the tablet in her lap. "Lots of questions for both Rasmussen and Sam." She ran her fingers through her hair and said, "I can understand why English majors may have an interest, but engineers and track-stars probably have no idea what an orchestra is."

"Don't be a snob. Einstein played Mozart on his violin. Very well, actually. Look at me; a computer nerd who's finding a touch of magic in music. We'll go after anybody who's warm."

Angie roared with laughter.

* * *

Woody slipped a floppy disc into his work computer while Angie stood over his shoulder. "You can't believe the hoops I had to jump through to get Gateway's student roster," she said. "Had to promise I'd use the information only for our Yale project. Signed all kinds of legal-looking papers."

"No matter; you got the data. Things are going to be much easier using this disc. Can you imagine entering all the names and addresses manually?" He tapped a couple of keys and the roster popped up on the screen. "There! Wasn't that easy?"

Angie's eyes widened. "Wow, just like that! Sure glad you talked me into getting it. How did you know about that floppy thing? Rasmussen was impressed that I even knew such a thing existed. I told him I was married to a computer guru." A puzzled expression spread across her face. "What now? Use the list to address envelopes by hand?"

Woody chuckled. "No way. I have a computer program that merges information from two sets of data automatically. It can print envelopes and letters all by itself. You musician types are totally out of touch," he joked.

"You forget; this whole thing is about music, not mysterious computer programs," she shot back with a grin. "What's next?"

"Well, I guess we compose a letter. It can be the same for everyone except for the salutation."

That night Woody made a brief catch-up phone call with his father to explain the latest scheme. "You won't believe this, Father, but Angie and I are going to reveal the magic of classical music to all the kids at her school, not just music-majors!"

"Lots of luck. Mozart and teens have never mixed."

"Got to run—we've a letter to come up with."

They hustled Quad to bed and worked past midnight coming up with the letter. Blurry-eyed, they proofed the final version:

Dear so and so,

Gateway Community College is pleased to invite you to an exciting musical event once every month. Arrangements have been made with the Yale University Orchestra to reserve up to twenty seats for Gateway students at any performance of their choice. The schedule for the present season is attached. Room permitting, you can attend more than one concert. As a special incentive, all who sign up will be given a Yale baseball cap. This is truly an amazing opportunity to enjoy a world-class orchestra free of charge.

To get tickets, Contact Mrs. Angela Lawrence at the Music Department offices.

Sincerely, Gateway Community College

The next day, both Dean Rasmussen and Sam approved the letter. The next step fell on Woody and his incredible merging program. As he'd predicted, with a few keystrokes the computer crunched addresses and salutations for 1,456 letters and envelopes and deposited them on a fresh floppy. Three days later, the Yale administration office set a big box filled with ready-to-mail letters in Woody's arms.

Then came the grunt work. Night after night Woody and Angie, with sporadic help from Quad, folded and stuffed. They were rewarded with aching shoulders and a fussy kid, but finally they stacked an immense pile of envelopes into a carton ready for postage. "Glad that Gateway is going to pay for the stamps," Woody said. "It'll cost over $350 bucks."

"At least we don't have to lick the damn things," Angie sighed. "School has a postage meter." She leaned back and rubbed her shoulder. "What now? The posters?"

"Let me help," Woody said as he scooted over and massaged her back. "Yeah, the Yale Art Department ginned up some snazzy posters for us," he said. "All we have to do is put them up."

Angie squirmed with pleasure under Woody's strong hands. "How did you get them to do that?"

"They do it all the time for their regular concerts. They just tweaked a design for us."

"Looks like we're almost there," Angie said cheerfully.

"Yup, we're in the starting blocks."

The next week, Angie enlisted two of her favorite students to put up posters. "We have only a dozen, so hang them where you think they'll do the most good." Remembering Woody's admonition to recruit anyone who's warm, she added, "Don't forget the science laboratories and the gym."

At that very moment, Woody dropped off the letters at the post office.

* * *

Responses flooded Angie's office—over fifty on the first day. Jubilant, Woody created a spreadsheet to track names and phone numbers, all sorted by performance. The Mozart program was followed by a Vivaldi night, then J.S. Bach… everything filled up fast. He snatched the phone and called Sam. "Hey, man, I've got dozens of students signing up. I'm turning people away because we're at the twenty-person limit. Can you bump that up to twenty-five or thirty?"

"Sorry, I can't. We blocked out your twenty and are selling everything else. Reserved seating, you know."

Shaking his head, Woody said, "Too bad. There's room on the buses for more, but I know concerts usually have a full house. We'll see if we can get the students to go on other nights."

Dean Rasmussen beamed his approval upon hearing Angie's news. "I've arranged a bus company to meet the group in the north parking lot. I assume you will ride with our students."

"My husband Woody too."

"No problem."

A week and a half later, a nervous Woody stood by the door of the bus with a checklist while Angie clutched an armload of baseball caps, handing them out. He nodded to a burly jock-looking guy. "Don't forget your hat. Welcome to Mozart."

"I don't know from Mozart." Jabbing his thumb at a stunning co-ed next to him he muttered, "She made me do it."

Woody glanced at the girl and chuckled. "You're a smart man. You might even enjoy the concert. They're doing Mozart's 40th Symphony, one of his most popular."

"Whatever." The guy put his arm around the waist of his honey and clambered into the bus.

As the students boarded, Woody checked them off his list, and soon all but one was accounted for. He looked anxiously about.

With a playful nudge, Angie said, "There's always one laggard. Simmer down; there's time."

At last, a skinny guy sprinted across the parking lot, puffing. "Sorry I'm late."

"Hi, Jason, hop in." As he did, Angie turned to Woody and whispered, "He's in my class. Plays violin in Gateway's orchestra."

The din in the bus pounded on Woody's ears, and he sighed with relief as it pulled up to the concert hall at Yale. As everyone filed off, he handed a ticket to each. "Follow Angie, er Mrs. Lawrence," he instructed.

Chatting loudly, the group jostled to their seats. Within minutes, musicians took their places onstage carrying their instruments and began tuning. Woody noticed the jock-guy in the next row holding his girl's hand and squirming uncomfortably.

Shortly, the conductor strode onto the stage and bowed to a burst of applause. Confused, the jock let go of his girl's hand and clapped awkwardly.

The conductor mounted the podium, rapped his baton on the music stand and Mozart's melodic opening notes soared lightly over the audience. Jason, Angie's student, waved his hands in little arcs as if conducting the passage himself. The jock, Woody noticed, bobbed his head in time with the music.

Mesmerized by the symphony, Woody took Angie's hand and forgot all but the phenomenal notes flowing from the stage.

The concert ended with thundering applause and cheers. The conductor, and then the orchestra, took bows as the applause went on and on.

Hand-in-hand, Woody and Angie jockeyed down the aisle and headed to the bus for the ride back to Gateway. Both tried to tune in on the conversations of the students, listening for praise or disappointment. Woody had to grin when the jock told his girlfriend that Mozart was "cool."

This prompted Woody to thread his way over. "I see you enjoyed the music."

"Yeah, man. Who'da thought."

"My name is Woody and I work with the orchestra. Your name?"

"Jack. Jack Trumbo."

"You plan to come to any more of these concerts? We take a group every month, you know."

Jack turned to his girlfriend and winked. "You can count on it, Woody."

"Super. See you next month." As he returned to Angie, a lump rose in his throat. *Another acolyte at the altar of Mozart. It's a fine thing you're doing, Woody.*

The bus eased into the Gateway parking lot and Angie stood. "Attention, everyone! Before you leave, I want to know what you thought of the concert. Whoever wants to go to another one, raise your hand." She gasped when nearly everyone waved at her. "Great! We're planning another trip back to Yale in four weeks, but we're almost at the limit. If you want to go, let me know right away. I'll be in my office if anyone wants to sign up tonight."

Nearly a dozen people, including Jack, followed her to the office where the next two concerts filled up immediately. Entering reservations on the computer, Woody shrugged and pointed at the screen. "Sorry, we can take only twenty at a time. Come back in a week or two and we'll see if we can fit you in down the line." He was greeted by groans.

After herding everyone out, Woody and Angie drove to her sister's to pick up Quad. There, Maureen put down her ledger and greeted them with a smile. "That boy! He's into everything. Eventually I got him to bed so I could finish the ledger for my latest customer." She pointed at a children's book on the floor. "I read to him. He liked the pictures, but then he started throwing his Lincoln Logs at the waste basket pretending it was basketball." She breathed a deep sigh. "But I love him dearly."

"You're a wonder, Sis," Angie said. "We don't know what we'd do without you."

"No problem. I have my own CPA business running from home, I can find time to help out. By the way, how was the concert?"

"You know; Mozart's the best," Angie gushed.

"Except for Beethoven," Woody corrected. "What was amazing, though, nearly all the students loved it. Or course most were in Angie's music appreciation class, but there was this buff-looking guy named Jack who…" Woody related the tale. "He came with his girlfriend and really liked the concert."

"Afterwards, we went to my office and made reservations for the next two concerts." Angie said. "Sold out! Everyone was really disappointed they couldn't get seats."

"Sounds really nice," Maureen said. "Look, I'm bushed. Let me get Quad and you two can go on your way."

"Let me," Woody insisted.

Fussing, the boy squirmed in Woody's arms while he tried to wrap a jacket around the tyke's shoulders. "Dang, the guy is getting heavy," Woody complained, setting his son beside him on the sofa. Quad, noticing he'd become the center of attention, giggled. "I want some ice cream, Daddy. Auntie doesn't have any."

Laughing, Angie said, "We'll fix you a small dish when we get home. Then it's beddy-bye."

Back at home, his tummy satiated by a cup of rocky-road ice cream, Quad instantly fell asleep, leaving Woody and Angie relaxing with a glass of wine. "What a day," Angie breathed. "I never would have guessed that Mozart would displace Bobbie Brown. I think your idea is a winner."

Woody bobbed his head in agreement and patted Angie's arm. "It's a crime we can treat only twenty students a month. There's gotta be a better way."

"We're stuck with the rules."

"I suppose, but I've never been one to be held back because of silly rules." His face screwed up in thought.

Angie reached over and hugged him. "Am I about to get into more trouble with another of your wild ideas?"

He stood and paced, rubbing his twitchy eye. "You know, there is more than one orchestra."

"Oh, my God. Now what?"

"The Boston Symphony Orchestra."

* * *

Shaking her head, Angie laughed. "It's crazy I know, Dean Rasmussen, but my husband is always coming up with crazy projects. He got so pumped up over the success of our trip to Yale's concert that skyrockets went off in his brain. He's crushed because we are turning away dozens of students every day. So, he conjured up this new scheme."

"I understand, but the Boston Symphony Orchestra? That's a commercial organization and it's a two-hour drive from here. I'm not sure our liability and vehicle insurance would even cover such an outing. Besides, how do you know that Boston would go along with it?"

"My husband got a name at the Boston Symphony from Sam Richter over at Yale. He's made an appointment to go see the assistant house manager tonight. He'll line up the orchestra and my job is to arrange bus transportation. Because it's for Gateway students, I think the insurance would cover it because it's an official school function. As for the commute, the Gateway students are basically adults. It would make for a super outing. Especially if we include a nice dinner en-route at some greasy spoon."

"Well, he hasn't convinced the Boston people yet," Rasmussen said. "Let me know if he actually does it."

Angie leapt to her feet. "My husband has unaccountably been swept up in classic music. He's mad about it. I'm positive his plan is a sure thing, but I'll drop in tomorrow and confirm."

A wry grin crossed the Dean's face. "If he convinces them, I'll be amazed. So, if you'll excuse me, I have work to do."

* * *

Tired from the long drive, Woody stood in front of the Boston Symphony Hall and admired the soaring columns bathed in the glow of the summertime setting sun. *Impressive, particularly to a computer geek.* He checked a note he'd written to make sure he remembered where the rear entrance was. Confident, yet nervous, he wheeled and strode around the edifice. He found a door labeled "Stage Entrance" and walked in. Folding chairs, music instrument cases, and tattered cardboard cartons lined the hall, but he saw nobody around. Puzzled, he took a few steps when an elderly lady tottered around a corner carrying a file folder. "May I help you?" she asked.

"You sure can. I have an appointment with Mr. Russell Zimmerman. He's the assistant house manager."

She waved her hands as if gently pushing Woody away and beamed. "Oh, you lucky man! Russ is a dream! Nicest man you'll ever meet. Let me put this file away and I'll show you to his office." After hunting around a bit, she slipped the folder into one of the boxes and turned. "Follow me."

Chuckling to himself, Woody followed the pert woman through a maze of passageways and storage rooms. At last, she said, "Here he is!" Judging from her gesture, she might have been introducing the King of England.

Through the open door, Woody saw a totally bald, middle-age man sporting a huge mustache and wearing checkered pants. "Ah, you must be Mr. Woodrow Lawrence," he said.

"Just call me Woody." Looking at the cartoon-like character behind the desk, he thought, *this is going to be a pushover.*

"And you can call me Russ. Take a seat."

"Thanks." Woody eased into an overstuffed chair covered in ancient scarred leather. "Thanks for taking time to see me."

"Not a problem, there's no performance today, so it's kicking-back time. Now then, you said something about bringing students from Gateway Community College to see some concerts. You work for Gateway?"

"No, I don't. Actually, I'm assistant manager of Yale's orchestra. In a nutshell, here's what we're doing now." Woody explained how he'd arranged for twenty students a month to attend Yale concerts. How popular it turned out to be. How he had to turn away dozens of students. How the local newspapers picked up on the story. How an athlete named Jack liked Mozart. "It's a crime that these students have no way to enjoy classical music. They're constantly bombarded by the likes of Michael Jackson and Eminem and listen to nothing else. I'm hoping that The Boston Symphony can help out."

"Anyone is free to buy a ticket."

"Look, they're in junior college. Money is a problem for most. So is transportation. As it is, Yale offers good seats free of charge and Gateway has contracted with a bus company. I thought you and I might work out a similar deal."

Russ crossed his arms. "We're really on a tight budget. All orchestras are. I don't see how we could help you."

Stunned, Woody gulped. "There has to be a way. Think of all the good publicity you'd get. Think about all the future customers you'd have."

"You can't imagine how often we're asked to give away seats, backstage tours, even music lessons. As it is, we have to rely mostly on federal and state grants to survive. Sometimes big rich businesses will sponsor a guest conductor or a special soloist, but that's it."

This guy's no pushover. "Could we get a grant or something?"

Russ shook his head and stroked his mustache. "We've pretty much used up all the possibilities. Sorry."

Woody hunkered down in thought. *Big rich companies. Sounds like Yale alumni.* "You've given me an idea,." He bounced from the chair, shook hands, and rushed through the door, eyelashes fluttering.

The Herald American
Monday, April 24, 1989

Massive Student Riots in China

Startled by the headline, Angie shook her head. At least our Gateway kids don't have problems like in Beijing. What a mess!" She set the paper down and swallowed the last bite of breakfast cereal. "Woody," she called out. "I have to get going. I've a meeting with the dean first thing to explain our situation."

"Yeah, I have to run too," he replied. "That Vivaldi concert for your students is right around the corner—gobs of work to do. Wish I could invite those Chinese students; they need to be rewarded for standing up to a suppressive regime. Like you said, what a mess."

* * *

"Sorry to say, Dean Rasmussen, it didn't work out like we wanted," Angie said. "The Boston Orchestra has a huge overhead which means they have to sell every seat just to break even. Unlike Yale, they don't seem sensitive to their community image." She shook her finger at him, making a point. "But Woody has another plan."

"Seems like he *always* has big ideas," Rasmussen grinned. "I guess I don't have to charter more buses just yet."

"Maybe not right away, but don't count us out. Woody has a way of making things happen. He's working like crazy on Yale's Vivaldi concert this Saturday and wants to do something special. The man even wants to invite those Chinese kids rioting in Tiananmen Square! No way, of course." Angie chuckled. "He *loves* Vivaldi and thinks the music would calm them down," she giggled. "That aside, we talked about last month's Mozart concert and decided I should have given a little pep talk on the bus. You know, give them a little insight into what they're about to hear. He's typing up notes to give me, so you'd think he was the music expert in the family. It's amazing how a mega-science guy can do such an about-turn. Classical music has become really important in his life."

"That sounds good." Rasmussen flashed a mischievous grin. "Let me know what is going on with his newest brainstorm, okay?" *Chinese rioters, really?*

* * *

Angie steadied herself on the front seat as the bus trundled toward Yale. In her other hand, she clutched notes she'd worked up using Woody's bullet points.

"Listen up everybody," She shouted over the drone of the engine. "Tonight we're going to hear some of Antonio Vivaldi's music. He lived in Venice, Italy during the seventeenth and eighteenth centuries, so the music was composed about two hundred and fifty years ago. An ordained priest, he gave up the church in favor of music. All told, he composed over 800 pieces—how's that! We'll hear part of his most famous piece, *The Four Seasons*. Very melodic. You'll love it. Also, we'll hear portions of *Gloria*. It has twelve movements, but they're only performing four of them. It's religious music featuring a small choir. The orchestra is small too, about the size of our Gateway orchestra. Vivaldi was a very accomplished violinist, so you'll hear lots of strings."

The bus pulled up and disgorged twenty chattering students while Woody and Angie herded them inside. As they clambered into their seats, Woody saw Jack Trumbo, nodded at him, and got a thumbs-up in return.

Stirred with *Gloria,* the students whispered between movements and gestured excitedly. They definitely enjoyed the closing performance of the *Four Seasons,* evidenced by their rapt attention. While Angie made mental notes for a talk on the way back to Gateway, Woody fell into an enchanted trance, buried in the music and oblivious of his surroundings.

When the last notes faded in the auditorium, the entire audience sighed in awe, and broke into a crescendo of cheers and clapping. The Gateway students appeared transformed and were slow to rise from their seats, chatting and gesturing. Woody and Angie prodded them toward the exit and counted heads as they boarded the bus.

"Okay, people, what did you think?" she called out.

Heads nodded and voices murmured. "Weird," yelled one. "Wow!" bellowed another.

Laughing, Angie asked, "How many of you have gone to a Gateway symphony performance or any orchestral concert?"

Less than a third of the hands went up.

"What did you think of *Gloria*? What about a choir singing alongside an orchestra?"

Both shrugs and broad smiles.

"Did anyone notice how complicated the music sounded?"

Nods.

"I'd like everyone to think about what you heard tonight and compare it to current popular music. Think about *Miss You Much* or *Look Away*. You think those two songs will still be played in two-hundred and fifty years?"

Laughter.

"No way," shouted Jack.

"Point made," Angie smirked.

That night Woody reveled in the memory of the performance. "I'll bet we opened up a new world for those kids today. A boxing match between Vivaldi and Michael Jackson—what a scene! Did you hear them talking about *The Four Seasons*? How they actually could hear winter or spring?" He stared into his glass of wine. "Only twenty people a month…we have to find a way to do better."

"You said you had an idea."

"You wait and see. Under my amazing power of negotiating, the Boston Symphony Orchestra will bow to our demands," he quipped.

* * *

Impatient, Woody dialed in the levels from the microphones that fed the tape recorder and fiddled to balance them properly. That night Yale was going to have a much-anticipated performance of Beethoven's *Ninth Symphony* led by a prominent guest conductor. He looked forward to comparing Beethoven's *Choral Symphony* with Vivaldi's *Gloria,* but he had urgent business with Sam first. At last, the setup fell into place and Woody strode toward his boss's office.

"Sam, I need to talk to you about an idea I have. Got a minute?"

"Are you nuts? The choir is running helter-skelter looking for robes while the orchestra's sheet music is all mixed up. Biggest night of the season and you want to talk about another of your *ideas?* No way. Come see me in the morning."

Woody's dejection didn't last long—that night the first notes of the *Ninth* floated into the wings where he monitored the quietly spinning tape recorder. Woody closed his eyes in ecstasy and he softly took Angie's hand, pleased that he got permission for her to be backstage. She too, became entranced.

Late that night, Woody was too mesmerized by the symphony to worry about what Sam would say about his ideas. The Ninth had bolstered his sense of music and moved him powerfully.

Sam trudged to his office the next morning, exhausted from the previous night's pressure. He found Woody waiting for him, tapping his foot.

"Before you get started, will you let me get a cup of coffee?" Sam moaned.

"Sure." Not willing to let his prey wander off, Woody followed him to the coffee machine around the corner saying, "I had this conversation with Russ Zimmerman…"

"So I understand. He asked if I knew you."

"So, you know?"

With a weary look, Sam settled in his office chair. "Yeah, but no details."

Woody rushed through his carefully planned spiel about his meeting with Zimmerman at the Boston Symphony. "As you know, all costs for trips to Yale are being taken care of by Gateway College. But Boston Symphony Orchestra, BSO for short, has to sell all their seats to meet costs. Even our kids would have to pay." He threw up his hands in exasperation. "But we have no money."

Sam slurped his coffee noisily. "You asking me for money?"

"I suppose a successful house manager like yourself could turn up with a few big ones," Woody joked, "but that's not what I have in mind."

Sam rolled his eyes. "Okay, tell me."

"Yale is an elite university that has gobs of famous, wealthy alumni like presidents Taft, Bush, and Ford. Even Samuel Morse of Morse Code fame was a Yale alum."

Sam looked at his watch. "Get to the point, will you?"

"I need a patron. Someone who'll buy tickets for the Gateway students. Not only that, but dinner in Boston at some nice restaurant too. I bet millions of bucks are donated to the University every year. I need to find a generous soul who'll pop for a grant to promote classical music—one who values kids. I don't know who to talk to. Can you tell me someone at Yale who handles grants so I can go see them?"

With a sigh of relief, Sam said, "That's easy. I believe Harry Coleman handles alumni matters. Talk to him; he's in the school directory."

Woody jumped up. "Thanks! I'll look him up today."

"Don't forget you're still working for me," Sam grumbled. "I need all the recording equipment put away and the tape delivered to security."

"I'm on it!"

* * *

That night, Woody hung up the phone with a scowl. "Father just can't let go of his lawyer fetish, Angie. He had no interest in helping us treat Gateway students to BSO concerts. He doesn't understand my newfound passion. He just bragged about how much money he's knocking down as an attorney."

Mischievously, he grabbed Quad and wrestled with him, tickling him into hysterics. Angie's eyes twinkled at the sight and she laughed. "Careful guys. You'll break something."

"Okay, Little Man, that's your mother's way of saying 'knock it off.' Run along, now. Your mother and I have some things to talk about."

With a concerned look, Angie asked, "You said Sam was mad at you? Any idea why?"

"He didn't seem mad, just grumpy. I'm guessing last night's production of *The Ninth* wore him out. He looked beat and he talked like he didn't have time or the energy to deal with another of my ideas. He'll be fine in a day or two; he just didn't appreciate my tactless interruption. All that doesn't matter—he gave me the name of a staff member who handles alumni affairs. Coleman's his name."

Angie slipped into her profound professor mode, flashing a sly grin. "The first step in your plan should be to find a moment when this Coleman person is between panics. And be calm. You can get too excitable sometimes."

Woody chuckled. "Excitable or enthused?"

"When it comes to you, dear husband, both words are euphemisms." She leaned back with a studied expression. "How do you plan to get ready for a meeting with Coleman?"

A shrug.

"What do you know about this guy?"

"Nothing."

"Pay attention—here's phase one of the plan. You have to find out all you can about him. Likes, dislikes, hobbies, years with Yale, all that. Especially what his official job entails."

"Sounds complicated. How can I do all that?"

"First, you find a day when Sam is mellow and buy him lunch. Schmooze him. And then subtly, very subtly, pick his brain about Coleman. To seal the deal, find something Sam mentioned in passing that he wanted done around the auditorium and do it before the meeting. Surprise him."

"Wow. You're making a lot of sense."

"There's more. Who is this Coleman fellow? To find out, buy him a lunch and thank him for taking time to see you. Tell him you're working to raise money to buy tickets for the students to attend concerts at BSO. Ask if he knows Sam. Bet he does; it's a tight community in the symphonic world."

His head swimming, Woody asked, "You done?"

"Nope. Who else at Yale, stage crew, or otherwise might know something? After talking with them, you sit down with me and we'll plot the coup d'état."

Woody shook his head in wonderment. He walked over to Angie, took her hands, and lifted her from her chair. "You're a devious, evil, witch and I love you beyond words." With that, he gave her a passionate kiss.

* * *

Dinner was over and Quad had been tucked into bed. Muted summer night sounds floated through an open window: crickets chirped and a truck growled softly in the distance. Angie raised a glass of wine in a toast. "This is a perfect setting to launch 'The Plan'. You've had ten days; what did you come up with?"

Woody toasted back, took a sip, and chuckled. "I found out that this Coleman guy is a nut-case. He started years ago as a history professor. He's written a couple of books on the Civil War—his passion. Collects war memorabilia by the ton. Sam says Coleman is about five-foot six and weighs 250 pounds and sucks up Italian food like crazy, particularly pizza. The head of the history department got frustrated because Coleman insisted on starting a special class just for Civil War weaponry. That, plus student complaints, got Coleman transferred to administration and alumni affairs."

"There's plenty of meat right there. Did you talk to Zimmerman?"

"Yup. He didn't know much about Coleman except he has a reputation for running in high society. He has season tickets to the Boston Symphony Orchestra and the ballet too. Has a girlfriend in downtown Boston, so he has a place to crash after a night at BSO. Often treats VIPs and donors to Yale's concerts. Zimmerman said Coleman really likes music, which fits right in while trolling for donors. Speaking of Zimmerman, he seemed more interested in my computer work at Yale than Gateway students. Weird."

Angie popped to her feet and paced. "Seems really simple. Here's what you do: take Coleman to the best pizza joint in town. Obvious, huh? Bone up on the Civil War— muskets, cannons, Generals Lee and Sherman. You're already up to speed on the orchestra, so mention that you understand he attends BSO and what might be his favorite composition."

"Pizza and music okay, but I hate history."

"You want money to buy tickets?"

Woody tipped his head and scowled.

"Then gush over the Civil War and what it meant to our country. See if he's a fan of President Lincoln. When he's nice and relaxed, ease into your scheme. Relate to what Coleman does to reel in donors. Say you're looking to follow his example." She tossed her hands into the air. "Simple."

"Except for Civil War history."

* * *

Coleman's office looked like a cross between a museum and a dump. The walls were covered with powder horns as well as swords and muskets. In contrast, all horizontal surfaces suffocated under piles of history books and all kinds of civil war memorabilia. A maze of boxes littered the floor and junk covered what appeared to be chairs. Coleman sat behind his inundated desk, beaming broadly. "Come in, come in," he called out to Woody. "Have a seat."

Walking up to the desk, Woody's face had a perplexed expression. There was no place to sit.

"Oh, just shove that stuff off the chair onto the floor," Coleman said. "My filing system is somewhat innovative."

"Thanks." Woody waved his hand at the wall. "Some kind of Civil War things you have." He launched into Angie's spiel, mostly asking questions rather than flaunting his meager knowledge about the war. He pointed to a rifle prominently displayed on the wall. "That is different from the others. What is it?"

"Sharp eye, young man. That's a Henry repeating rifle. Very advanced for the time."

After a few minutes of chit chat, Woody said, "Say, I'm hungry and it's nearly lunch time. You?"

"I'm always ready for some chow. Cafeteria?"

"You know, I'm in the mood for pizza. There's a great place within walking distance." *(Angie found it in the yellow pages).*

"Ah, you're thinking of Peppe's Pizza Parlor. I know it well."

Thus, it happened—pepperoni, checkered tablecloths, and chilled steins of beer fulfilled

Woody's dream. "No reason to line up a special grant," Coleman said, "I know a very generous patron who supports the arts, particularly our symphony orchestra. Let me get with him and explain your program for the Gateway kids. He'll love it! Why, he'll just peel off a few of the big ones from his regular donations and buy tickets and dinners for you. Small potatoes compared to his usual contributions! I'll call him this afternoon and get back to you no later than tomorrow. It's a sure thing."

Back at work that afternoon, Woody looked up Angie first thing and boasted about the news. Feigning a bored look, she said, "Of course. I knew what would happen all along."

Woody hugged her. "You're an amazing seer."

Woody felt ecstatic as he bent over the computer while working up a sequence for lighting and recording queues. Sam glanced in and nodded his approval over Woody's industry.

That night, his joy was infectious; his tickling sent Quad into hysterics. The melee came to an end when Angie called them to dinner. The telephone interrupted their banter and wild joking between bites of food.

"It's for you," Angie said, handing the receiver to Woody while calming Quad.

"Hello?"

"This is Zimmerman. Have a moment?"

"Oh, Mr. Zimmerman? What can I do for you?" A strange look crossed Woody's face. "Well, when there are no performances, I normally work until five. Why do you ask?"

The voice on the phone murmured something.

"Tomorrow night?" Woody asked. "Let me think. No, I don't have anything going on." His brow wrinkled in thought. "I suppose I could take off work a little early. Why do you ask?"

Woody pressed the phone to his ear. "You want to talk tomorrow? Seven o'clock in your office? Really? It's a long drive, but… What's it about? Well… Sure, can do."

Woody's eyebrows drew together as he listened intently. "Oh, okay. Until then, goodbye." He set the phone in the cradle.

Puzzled, Angie asked, "What is all that about?"

"Weird. Zimmerman at the BSO wants to talk with me tomorrow night. Wouldn't say why. Gonna be a long drive, but he was insistent."

"Maybe it's about the Gateway students attending their concerts."

"Not sure. If that's the case, why didn't he say so?"

* * *

With a jovial look on his face, Zimmerman twisted his mustache and waved Woody into a chair. "I remember you saying you worked at Yale University as assistant manager for their orchestra."

"Yeah; that's right."

"You like your work?"

"Sure do. It's kinda exciting, hanging around all the performers. Sometimes big names come in as soloists." Woody grinned. "I run the electronics just off the stage. I have a ringside seat to all their events. Can't beat that."

Zimmerman frowned. "And you're also involved with those Gateway kids, right?"

"You bet. Guess you heard that I located a Yale patron to buy BSO tickets for them."

"Yes, I did. You must think a lot about our Boston Orchestra."

"Oh, it's the best! World famous!"

"I'll get straight to the point. What do you know about this letters-on-the-computer thing?"

Confused by Zimmerman's change in direction, Woody stammered, "You mean email? Been around for a few years. Really getting popular. Why do you ask?"

"Our organization is struggling with it. We have a semi-retired math professor managing our web activity and computer system. Candidly, he's stuck in the fifties. We need help."

Woody raised a quizzical eyebrow. "Okay?"

"More and more performers and venues are inquiring about it—you said it's called email?"

"Yeah, right" Woody blurted. "I've been piddling around with it and I'll tell you; it's the wave of the future."

Zimmerman stroked his mustache. "We've been doing a little digging around about you at Yale. They say you're a talented young man when it comes to computers."

"Not bragging or anything, but I ought to be. Cut my teeth on the very first Apple II. It's been, what, a dozen years or so?"

"At Yale, what are you doing to improve their computer capabilities going forward?"

"Like I said, it's email time. I've also been creating better programs to track performance schedules, production needs, and publicity. I even have a crazy idea about setting up a spot on the computer so anybody can look up information about Yale's orchestra—who's performing, guest conductors, maybe even buy tickets right on the computer. There's no end to it."

Zimmerman leaned back in his chair with a serious expression. "How would you like to work for me, Woody? It sounds like you could do a lot for us."

Taken aback, Woody gasped. "I haven't given any thought about changing jobs. I have lots of friends at Yale and there's the program for the Gateway people. But I have to admit that Yale isn't all that interested in expanding their computer capabilities. I have to push them, you know."

"I can make you a very generous offer. We want to get into more radio broadcasts and television too. I understand you also manage all the recording efforts at Yale. I see a real fit.

"The Boston Pops is a whole other thing—we play at Tanglewood during the summer. Outdoors, you know which requires special equipment and set-ups. But there's something else. Unlike Yale, we rarely perform overseas. So if you're interested in traveling…"

"I've turned down London and Tokyo gigs with Yale," Woody replied, "because I have a young son and the babysitting thing is a chore. I'm too busy with family and Gateway to take off."

"Fine." Zimmerman patted a manila folder on his desk. "I don't expect an answer right now. You'll probably need to relocate to Boston, so it's a big decision. This is a packet I've put together explaining the scope of the job, insurance, and benefits. Look it over and get back to me within a day or two. If this information seems interesting, we'll get together and talk salary."

Stunned, Woody took the folder and said, "I thought you wanted to talk about the Gateway students attending your concerts. This is a huge surprise."

"You have a special set of skills, Woody. Not often do I encounter a computer expert with a passion for classical music. I'm convinced we'd build you a comfortable, but challenging nest right here in BSO." He shifted in his chair and tugged his mustache again. "One other thing. Before you go, I'd like to explore your idea about that spot on a computer where customers can buy tickets."

"Wouldn't that be something? What do you want to know?"

An hour later, Woody tucked the folder under his arm and breezed out the door, his head swirling with innovative projects he could conjure for BSO.

* * *

Angie had been jotting a few notes on a pad late that night when Woody burst in shouting, "I have big news! Sit down while I tell you about it!"

She jerked herself around and said, "No way! I'm going first because my news is bigger than your news!"

"Can't be."

"Shut up and listen, damn it. Rasmussen called me into his office and told me he's going to miss my excellent work. I was puzzled to say the least. 'Am I fired?' I asked. He laughed. He went on to say Gateway is getting together with other community colleges to form an association to promote the arts. They've asked me to be the college district's Cultural Emissary! They are also teaming with schools in Massachusetts so I'll have to travel all over both states working with administrators to create new programs, doing outreach to high school kids, and all that." She whirled like a dancer and cried out, "I'm so excited!"

"That's incredible!" Woody cried.

"And a huge pay increase too! All my travel expenses will be reimbursed! I'll even have a secretary. Beat that, Mr. Hotshot."

Quad, wakened by the racket in the other room, came running to investigate. "What's all the yelling about?"

Angie swept him into her arms. "Mommy got a big promotion at work. We're excited!"

Woody jumped from his chair, embraced them both, and smothered Angie with kisses. "Today is a day that will set records in the annals of the Lawrence family history. Let me tell you my news, Miss High-and-Mighty. Zimmerman, the guy at the Boston Symphony, gave me this folder after a long talk about computers. Here, check it out." With a satisfied smirk, he leaned back and watched Angie read, her eyebrows rising by the minute.

Sleepy, Quad retreated to his room.

"You're going to be the BSO's computer expert?" Angie asked. "Run their data department? That's marvelous!"

"Like you, I expect a monstrous pay raise *if* I accept the offer. No secretary, but maybe an assistant or two. I won't be lugging music stands around, but I'll help design stage layouts and scenery as well as manage all the radio and TV broadcast stuff. Moreover, while you're flitting about, I'll have time to play catch with our son because BSO doesn't tour. Also, they'll throw in twenty free tickets to all the concerts for Gateway pupils. That, with Yale's patron, we'll treat forty people at a time! So there, my exalted executive, who has the biggest news?"

Laughing, Angie said, "It would be a tie except I have one other bit of news. That football looking guy who came to the Vivaldi concert?"

"Yeah. His name is Jack Trumbo. What about him?"

"He's going to sign up for my music appreciation class."

"Hot damn!" High fives terminated a very late evening.

Woody made another trip to Boston and negotiated a handsome salary. "I'm sorry to cherry-pick Yale," Zimmerman said, "but you'll have lots of opportunity here to develop your skills and move BSO into the future."

A firm handshake sealed the deal.

Rejoicing in the exciting vision of their futures, the next night they celebrated at one of the most elegant restaurants in town, ordering lobster and French champagne while Quad quaffed a burger.

* * *

Like wolves chasing a rabbit, they barreled into their new roles. Surprisingly, even Woody's father seemed impressed with the news. In a panic, Woody took a motel room in Boston while Angie traveled to Hartford to meet with the newly formed committee to draft a charter for the organization. Luckily, Maureen took Quad under her wing. Woody, miffed because the BSO used IBM's PnP ISA computers rather than Apples, dove into an entirely strange operating system and devoured programs like Excel 5.0 and Word 6.0. One of his first tasks involved scheduling production activities, which agitated him. Like a horse chomping on the bit, he hungered to work on the new passion in his life: the development of a computer site where patrons could learn about the orchestra and buy tickets directly.

Back home late that weekend, Angie struggled through the front door tugging on her small suitcase. Woody greeted her with a small bouquet of roses and a glass of wine. "Tell me all about Hartford."

With a sigh, she collapsed in her easy chair and inhaled the fragrance of the flowers. "It was great. Two days of really intense discussions. Each college has their own specialties; the school in Stamford for instance, is trying to lure businesses to compensate for the economic downturn. So they push the business curriculum, but even so, their school has a good music program. On the other hand, Quinsigamond in Massachusetts supports their big annual music festival, but also has business concerns." She tossed her hands in the air. "We all agreed that the arts are suffering in this recession—no money, low priority."

"Giving up?"

"Hell, no! We had a lot of good ideas; we just have to figure ways to carry them out." She turned to the flowers Woody had brought. "They're lovely." She took a sip of wine. "Where's Quad?"

"Did your watch stop working? It's nearly midnight; he's in bed."

"I *have* lost track of time. Sorry. Tell me how things are going at the BSO."

"It's a big operation for sure. They've got me jumping through hoops. Making plans for the visit by the Gateway people is one of my top priorities. During the evenings, I started looking for a nice apartment for us. Are you sure the community college district will be okay if you relocate to Boston? After all, your work will be both in Connecticut and Massachusetts. That means you can't teach your classes."

"I know. By the way, that Trumbo fellow is tackling music as if it were a halfback." She drew a breath. "Back to my new job, they said there's no problem if I move. I'll just have to get used to driving a lot, but it will be only one or two trips a month."

"Suits me. I'm anxious to find a place so I can settle down and work on my pet idea. It's going to set the world on fire."

"That's the special page on the computer?"

"Right. It's complicated. I'm going to have to spend gobs of hours on it. That means more than a few late dinners. That okay?"

Angie patted his hand. "I'm thinking tonight is the perfect example: when I'm on the road you can rush home, feed Quad and then pound on your computer."

Woody grimaced. "Guess that means I'll have to get one of those funny IBM jobs."

"That, or borrow one from BSO."

Four months whirled by and they finally settled into a quaint apartment in Brookline. Their unit was on the third floor and featured a balcony view of the neighborhood and a niche with bay windows where Woody set up his office.

Thus, their new lives lurched along.

The Herald American
Friday, January 7, 1993
Section D1: Entertainment

Dizzy Gillespie Dies

World Morns Jazz Great

Home after a tough day at work, Woody thumped his fist on the arm of his chair and tossed the newspaper on the floor. *I'm not a big jazz fan, but it's sad when a legend like Dizzy passes away. Today, the world is a little smaller.* His grief was shuttled aside by the doorbell. Upon opening the door, he found Mary, their new babysitter, standing arms akimbo with a scowl on her lips. Without asking, she brushed snow from her shoulders and stepped into the house, tugging on Quad's arm.

"You asked if I could take care of your son this evening, but I have a life, you know. I adore Quad and enjoy watching him, but this is getting out of hand. Daytime is okay during the week, but this night stuff is too much. You've got to find someone else to care for him."

Woody hung his head. "I know I take you for granted, Mary, and I apologize. We've tried other babysitters and they never last. Quad's too much for them, I guess. We had the same problem in New Haven. I'll figure something out."

"Good."

He didn't tell Angie about the confrontation and decided to check out Boston agencies for help, but was astonished at the rates they charged. *Agencies rake off thirty percent of the fee – didn't have that problem having Mary. She's our good friend, but we took advantage of her when she babysat.* Desperate to find a way to work on his pet project, a peculiar idea came to his mind—his father. He realized his father had been cool toward him at the wedding, but obviously had connected with Quad. When Woody dropped out of Yale and rejected a career in law, their relationship became poisoned. Since then, they'd hardly spoken, just a terse phone call to him every month or so. As Angie had predicted, a grandson had an impact on Woodrow. From time-to-time he dropped in and spent time with Quad and Angie, but largely ignored Woody.

Father is semi-retired by now and maybe he's mellowed in his old age. What do I have to lose if I call? Besides, he's still a grandfather and is missing almost all of Quad's childhood. That could be an easy start to the conversation.

He waited until Angie took a trip to Bridgeport, another of her committee meetings, before picking up the phone. "Hi, father. It's me, Woody—er Woodrow. How are you doing?"

"Things are fine. What do you want?"

Evading the question, Woody said, "I thought you'd like to spend more time with Quad. He's growing up fast, you know."

After a pause, "I can imagine. Woodrow the Fourth is what? Nine?"

"Yeah. Time flies, doesn't it?"

"You call him Quad, don't you? Weird name. He told me he's not in soccer or Little League, right?"

"No. Seems like our careers got in the way. I'm sure you know that Angie's taken a position at the College District as a cultural emissary coordinating all the community colleges in

Connecticut and Massachusetts? She's away a lot. And my job at the Boston Symphony Orchestra is really working out. Like I said, in charge of all their computer operations, broadcasting, work on set design, stuff like that."

"I would never have guessed you two would be moving up in the world so quickly. I have to admit, I'm impressed. Who takes care of the Fourth while you two are knee-deep in work?"

"We had a friend but she's burned out. Quad—the Fourth I should say, is getting a little rambunctious. Maybe he pushed the sitter a little too much. So, I've been looking at several agencies to hire a baby-sitter part-time. Boy, it's expensive." Wondering if his father would take the hint, Woody said nothing.

"You probably didn't know that I retired some three months ago," Woodrow said. "Things are really boring. There has to be more to life than staring at the TV. I really miss the law."

Woody drew in a deep breath. *There it is – on the table.* "How about getting into the grandfather business? Your grandson really enjoys those rare times you show up."

"What do you mean? Throwing a baseball around with him? Trips to the zoo?"

"Well, maybe. Or just hanging out. Going fishing. The kid has never been fishing. Teach him about law." Woody chuckled. "Just joking."

"My bones are too old for all that, although my doctor wants me to lose some weight and exercise more. Does the little guy like baseball?"

"He probably doesn't know," Woody said. "Angie and I have no use for sports of any kind. By the way, he's grown an inch or two since you've been here."

"Let me think." Several moments passed by. "Tell you what, why don't I drop by some afternoon soon. I can take him out for a burger and ice cream. Wouldn't hurt for the Fourth to get to know his grandfather a little better. It *has* been awhile."

Woody pumped his fist while squelching a whoop of joy. "Sounds really great. I'll talk to Angie as soon as she returns from Bridgeport. I'm sure she'll have no objection."

"Great. I could use a little more racket in my life."

* * *

"I'll be up on the train, Woody," Woodrow said. "I'll rent a car, so there's no need to pick me up."

After such a long absence, that first meeting with his father could have been worse, Woody decided. It began very awkwardly in their cluttered apartment with Quad hovering at Woody's side, standing awkwardly first on one foot then the other. Looking to break the silence, the old man, Gramps, as he elected to be called, had given Quad a box labeled "Bump N' Go Action Robot." Shrieking with excitement, Quad had ripped open the box and chased the toy around the living room like a typical nine-year-old. "Got a winner there, Gramps," Woody had said.

Smiling, Angie stood to one side and watched her husband try to reconnect with his father.

For fifteen minutes, they exchanged pleasantries when Gramps announced he'd treat

Quad to a hamburger at a nearby entertainment complex featuring go-karts and pinball machines. Woody stood on the porch and watched the two hustle through the mild winter afternoon to the rental car.

As he scurried back to his computer to work on his latest idea, Woody felt a twinge of guilt for ditching his son. Hopeful his father had abandoned his surly ways and mellowed out, he settled behind the keyboard and screwed up his face in concentration. *First things first,* Woody thought. *Who's going to want a special page on someone else's computer? Probably mostly businesses.*

Two hours, filled with flashing insights and bold programming, slid into history. Woody didn't notice when Angie lugged two grocery bags into the kitchen and began making nesting noises. Later, she peeked into his "office" and said, "I guess Quad is still out with your father, right?"

"Yeah." The tapping of the computer keys continued without interruption.

She shrugged and started back to the kitchen when the front door banged open and Quad barreled over to his mother. "I'm the world's best racecar driver!" he screamed. "That's what I want to be when I'm older."

Grinning, Woody's father trailed behind the raucous boy. "Kid has a talent for sure. Couldn't get Quad away from those go-karts. He was passing everyone."

Distracted by the racket, Woody pressed "save" on the computer and went to see how well his father had gotten along with his son. Smiles all around told him all he needed to know. Looking at his boy, Woody had to grin. An untied shoelace along with smears of catsup and ice cream on his un-tucked shirt completed a Norman Rockwell image of a happy youngster.

"You should have seen me, dad! What do they say? Pedal-to-the-metal? That was me! There was a guy who tried to go around, but I cut him off at the sharp turn. Never had a chance."

"He wanted to drive the car back home," Woody's father chuckled. "I asked Quad if he knew the route, but he didn't. So, I suggested maybe I'd better take the wheel."

"Not fair," whined Quad. "You could have just pointed the way."

Laughing, Angie took her son by the arm. "Let's get you cleaned up, mister. Dinner is almost ready."

"You staying for dinner, Gramps?" Woody asked.

"It's nice that you ask, but I'm worn out. That kid has more energy than a team of horses—could hardly keep up. How about a rain check?"

"Sure thing." Hoping to get back to his project, Woody was secretly relieved.

"Leaving already?" Angie said as a spit-and-polished Quad skipped behind her.

"As I explained to Woodrow, er Woody, I'm bushed." He reached over and tousled Quad's hair. "Suppose you and I do go-karts again, okay?"

"Tomorrow?"

With a wink, Woodrow, now known as Gramps, said, "You know, let me check my calendar."

After a quick meal, Woody left Quad with the TV and Angie unpacking the few remaining groceries. He caressed his keyboard until midnight.

* * *

Woody's program began to take shape. Because of his sudden leisure, Gramps became a regular fixture: taking Quad to the zoo, back to ride the go-karts, and any movie featuring cowboys. But complications arose: Angie's business travels proliferated and Quad's school let out for the summer. Luckily, Gramps negotiated a deal on a nearby apartment and moved in, pleased to step into the breach. He often stayed for dinner and chitchatted with his daughter-in-law.

Woody worked feverishly late into the night and it was past ten when Angie staggered into his office. "What a trip. New Haven's Board of Alders is setting up a music festival weekend with marching bands, choral performances, and orchestral events. We had ten-hour meetings followed by protracted business dinners. I'm wiped out." Noting that Woody hardly looked up from the computer, she asked, "How is it going? Before I left, you said the new program was nearly finished."

A few wordless moments went by and then Woody jumped from his chair and violently threw a Coke bottle across the room, gouging a hunk of plaster from the wall. "Story of my god-damned life," he bellowed. "Should have done some research first!"

Startled, Angie stammered, "What's wrong?"

His face contorted in agony, Woody whimpered, "It's already out there. Websites they call them. More than a year ago, CERN, something to do with atomic energy, came out with a program to share information. I checked just now and there are already a thousand websites out there. All my work is wasted. I'm a damned Johnny-come-lately! Again!" He dropped to his knees and pounded the floor.

Angie knelt beside him and put her arms around his shoulders. "You're saying there is something that already promotes orchestras and lets you buy tickets on the spot?"

"I…I don't know." His shoulders heaved in misery. "This whole thing was my idea. A bunch of mad scientists stole it!"

"How can that be? You said they introduced it over a year ago."

Woody banged on the floor again. "I don't know. It seems like every time I get excited about something, it turns into a disaster. I'm done. No more fancy schemes for me. What's Russ going to think? All this time I've been pumping him up about how I'm going to put BSO in the headlines. He'll think I'm a jerk."

Angie pulled him to his feet and gave him a warm hug. "Okay, you didn't have the first website, whatever you call it, but why not make a special one just for our orchestra? Capitalize on CERN's stuff. Impress Russ with a program where patrons can purchase tickets right from their own computers. Like you said, it should be really easy, huh? There is a saying out there that failure is not the end of the road: it's a detour toward success."

Woody's clutched fist relaxed somewhat as Angie gently hugged him. He sucked in a huge breath and sighed. He rose slowly to his feet and paced with a odd expression on his face. "Detour, huh? Why just tickets?" he sniffed. His face screwed up in concentration as he strode back and forth. "Why not present performances right on their computer screens? World-wide." A devious looking smile spread across his cheeks and an eyelid fluttered. "A customer in London could buy a pass and watch BSO play Beethoven right from their living room. Gateway students wouldn't have to ride the bus anymore and colleges all over the world could tune in."

An immense gasp of relief escaped Angie's lips. "That sounds more like the Woody I fell in love with. You'll be an inspiration for me and Quad once more."

The Herald American
Saturday, September 7, 2002
<u>Section E1: Obituaries</u>

Woodrow Sterling Lawrence Jr.
1930 – 2002

Dynamic Founder of Prominent Law Firm

Community Leader Set High Standards

The reception hall echoed with the murmurings of 175 mourners. Woody, seated on the dais at the head table, looked out over the crowd. "Seems like father had some kind of following. I've never seen this many Brooks Brother suits in my life. The lawyer business has to be a rich one."

"Now don't get judgmental," Angie admonished. "I know you don't hold attorneys in high regard, but these people are here for your father."

"Yeah, give it a rest, Pop," Quad said. "Gramps wasn't an ogre. Remember he put the arm on Yale admissions and got me accepted just last month. I can't tell you how grateful I am. He and I actually became buddies after that go-kart day ages ago. I have a lot of respect for him even though he could be a real grump sometimes."

"I know, I know," Woody muttered. "He and I sort of got along these past few years. We simply fought over my career choice. He couldn't understand why anyone would turn away from Yale Law."

Quad grinned. "Well, he certainly talked me into it."

"Your choice. I had hoped you'd get into science but…"

"Come on, Pop, you had one science project after another blow up in your face. At least nowadays, you've pretty much adapted all that technology so you can spend your time working at BSO sneaking around listening to their music."

"Quad's right, you know," Angie said. "You hang out at the concert hall for hours. Running all the recording equipment is your excuse to hang out in the wings listening to rehearsals and performances."

With a wave of his hand, Woody said, "I have to admit that classical music has taken hold of me." Smiling, he slapped the table and said, "Enough of all this; I was finally getting to know my father and he up and dies of a heart attack at only seventy-two. I'm going to miss the old guy."

* * *

Quad stepped out of Yale's admissions office clutching a thick bundle of paper. He found a bench in the bright fall sun and shuffled through pamphlets, his class schedule, and handouts from various people running for school offices. One flyer in particular caught his attention: *Sign up for lacrosse in the gymnasium, Monday September 23rd*. He searched his memory for how lacrosse was played. He'd recalled how he'd been surprised that it's a contact sport where the players wore helmets and pads like football. Although well built in an athletic way, Quad was too small for football and baseball bored him to tears. Even though the notice interested him, Quad decided to skip the weird sport thinking: *First things first. Not going to screw up like Pop did.* Moments later he briskly walked to his first class at Yale, American history.

And so, his first year at the university passed—intense and single-minded. He took up lodging in one of the residential colleges, hoping that life there would be focused on academics rather than social stuff. He breathed a sigh of relief when his new roommate shook hands and silently returned to his studies. Quad frequented the library and professor's offices yet found time for several dates where he lost his virginity in a burst of lust rather than affection. He forced himself to return home once a month to be interrogated by Woody and Angie.

* * *

Woody stood on the porch and waved as Quad jumped into his car to return to Yale. He turned and took Angie's hand saying, "He never has much to say to us, does he? He's always so serious."

"I guess we're lucky to see him at all. Talks of nothing but his damn school work." Angie said.

"I'm seriously put out because he wouldn't join us to see the Wagner and Tchaikovsky concert next week at BSO. The end of the spring term is right around the corner, but is he going to take the summer off? Hell, no. He's signed up for summer session."

"He's certainly single-minded," Woody said. "I'd hoped to share my passion for music with him and the BSO program will be special; it's a combination of melodic and dramatic. 'No time,' he keeps saying."

"Well, he should take time. He's turning into a boring young man."

Woody nodded. "I don't get it. As a kid, he was rambunctious, into everything, a perky holy terror. But now…"

"Did you notice how he clammed up when I asked about his love life?"

"Yeah," Woody chuckled. "Same answer—'no time.' And his roommate? 'We don't bother each other,' he said. College is supposed to be a world expander, but he's holed up like a gopher in its hole."

"We'll see if his sophomore year will bring changes. He mentioned an interest in lacrosse, whatever that is." Angie shrugged.

"It's some kind of sport they play in college. Not like the NFL or MLB. No matter, it's not like music. Sports go away when you get older, but music is for life. My biggest regret is it took me so long to appreciate the glory of classical music." He gathered Angie in a warm hug. "You, my love, gave me Beethoven."

With a lecherous smile, Angie said, "You know, *Angie's Raft* is still hanging around. After all these years, I believe it is in need of a goddamn safety inspection."

* * *

The next two years flew by for Quad. He hadn't settled into Yale, he conquered it. Not just perfect grades, but student government and lacrosse as well. He joined the debate team and set new standards for excellence. His eyes were focused on becoming a flawless Yale man, and he succeeded. Classmates looked up to him and sought his opinion. Professors secretly celebrated if Quad enrolled in their classes. He lacked only one thing: female romance.

That changed the first week of his senior year when he attended a party for lacrosse players—both the men and women's teams. It began with backslapping, manly hugs, and boisterous greetings. As the star player, his presence was sought by everyone, including a new feisty player on the women's team. Her name was Sheri. Tall and lithe, she moved with the grace of a cheetah. Her laughter rang like sarna bells and her eyes twinkled and flashed in merriment. She planted herself firmly in front of Quad and said, "I hear you're a decent lacrosse player, but what happened at the debate with Wesleyan University? Got thumped pretty good." Sheri's wide grin betrayed her put-on disdain.

"That was a fluke—I had a bad cold." A bit of Quad's normal bravado wavered as he struggled for a better explanation, but her sparkling hazel eyes framed by long blond hair befuddled him.

"From what I'm told, you were named after the big lawn area in the center of campus. True?"

"What are you talking about?"

"You're called Quad, right?" Sheri giggled.

"Oh, I get it. Not that kind of quad. I'm Woodrow Lawrence the Fourth. My parents nicknamed me Quad."

"Clever. What are you doing tonight?"

Taken aback, he muttered, "Having dinner with you?"

"Aha, a stroke of genius! That will be at the Golden Rooster Grill, right?"

Speechless, Quad nodded sheepishly.

Some might call it a whirlwind, but that would be an understatement. Words better suited might be tornado, hurricane, or atomic blast. That spring they celebrated Quad's graduation and acceptance into Yale Law with an extravagant wedding.

The Herald American
Tuesday, October 23, 2012

RECORD VIEWERS for PRESIDENTIAL DEBATE

Woody set down the newspaper and sipped his morning coffee. "Looks like Obama is a shoo-in," he said to Angie. "I've become more interested in politics ever since Quad and Sheri started working the elections."

"I don't know where our son finds time to do everything," Angie said. "He just became a partner in one of the most prestigious law firms in the state and spends untold hours working for that weirdo state senator who's up for reelection. And Sheri has been elected to the school board. She was the one who got Quad interested in politics, you know. That's their life: Republicans against Democrats, right vs. left. I wish they'd work on getting a couple of grandkids for us."

Woody chuckled. "You and I got a fairly early start when a little carelessness kicked our butt, but we gave up after only one. Careers and silly ideas got in our way. Both of them are so busy I doubt they're even considering kids. When they hit their late thirties, they might wake up. In any event, it's not up to us."

"A new subject," Angie said. "How is your new position working out? It's been months since you became operations manager." She tucked her feet under her as if she expected a long answer.

"Boy, is it different. Like I've said, I hardly spend any time on the computer any more. I'm thick with our conductor and spend hours with him reviewing upcoming concerts. Now that fall is here, we've set aside plans for Tanglewood, but come early spring we'll dive back into it. Plenty to do with the winter performances—you can't believe how involved they get. Just finished preparations for another Gateway visit and I just hired a good technician to handle the recordings and radio broadcasts. Big load off my days. Along with the conductor, I sit in on auditions and screen tapes of other orchestral performances. Spending hours looking for potential works to do at BSO. It's crazy."

"But you love every goddamned minute of it, right?"

"They actually pay me to listen to music! I never imagined life could be so fantastic."

Angie playfully fondled one of Woody's stuffed kittens he'd given her. "Are you going to get off work this Sunday to go see the Melrose Symphony perform Dvořák's New World?"

"I've already cleared it—good to go. That should be a special evening because they're an all-volunteer orchestra. The word is they're really good."

"You're amazing. It wasn't that long ago you were a computer fanatic and a science geek. Now look at you. We're traipsing all over the state attending concerts. Last week it was the North Side Philharmonic, before that the Waltham Symphony. We have an exciting life, Woody."

He reached over and took Angie's hand. "My love for you gave me love for classical music. Like you've said before, as long as there are ears to hear,

Beethoven and Mozart will be played. On the flip side, World War II fighter planes went to junkyards with the advent of jets, and Isaac Newton has been shoved aside by Einstein who in turn will certainly fall prey to a better genius. You ever wonder what became of Edison's record player? Science is like a heroin rush; a Strauss waltz is forever."

As agreed, Woody and Angie drove to see the Melrose Symphony perform Dvořák's *New World symphony*. They settled into their seats just as the house lights went down. A burly man in a tux strode out on the stage and announced, "Tonight we have a dazzling performance of one of the most popular pieces of music ever. Before we begin…"

Woody gasped. "That's Jack Trumbo," he whispered. "What is he doing here?"

Angie thumbed through the program. "Ah," she murmured pointing to a line on the page. "Mister Jack Trumbo, Manager, Melrose Symphony."

"I'll be damned," Woody breathed.

The Herald American
Monday, February 4, 2019
Section C2: Technology Today

Hubble Telescope in Trouble Again

Scientists Search for Solutions

The clatter of sleet pelting the window drew Woody from his groggy slumber. He tried to roll over and cover his ear, but the tangled oxygen tube frustrated his efforts. Weak winter sunlight diluted the morning darkness and silhouetted the IV stand, making it look like a hideous alien. Suddenly, a sharp pain jabbed at his chest. He reached for the call button, but just as suddenly, the clutching agony went away. He breathed a deep sigh. T*hey won't do anything anyway. Why bother*? He glanced at the wall clock and remembered that Angie promised to drop by early that morning. *I'm not the man she married for sure. This is 2019 for crying out loud. They're supposed to have a cure for heart failure by* *now. I'm only fifty-nine, a young man by most standards. Well, not elderly anyway.*

A nurse sporting a grouchy frown barged into the room. Woody silently endured her fussing as she switched out an IV bag, took his temperature, and told him he was doing fine.

Yeah, right. What she really means is I'm still warm.

He spent the next hour staring at the ceiling, watching the clock, and waiting for Angie. He finally nodded off, lulled by the soft beeps of the monitors.

Later, Angie crept into the room and sat alongside Woody's bed, taking care not to wake her husband. Looking haggard, she lifted a book from her purse and began to read. Unaware, she didn't realize her presence and the rustling of the turning pages stirred Woody from his shallow dozing.

"Glad you're finally here. Had a bad night."

She reached over and patted his hand. "Didn't mean to wake you. Bad night you said?"

"I spent most of the night thinking about things, not sleeping."

"What sort of things?" Angie asked.

"Oh, you know; what did I do with nearly six decades of my life? Not much seems to come to mind at the moment."

"Don't be silly. They still talk about how your BSO website became a true breakthrough in the computer world. I remember Russ crediting you for saving the orchestra during the crappy recession of 2001. All the arts went into the tub back then except BSO. Your website pulled in revenue from all over the world. It was wonderful!"

"Well, it *did* get me that big promotion and a welcome raise. But now my website no longer has any use—obsolete."

"Well, that's progress. I remember you telling me what Sir Isaac Newton once said; 'If I have seen further, it is because I stand on the shoulders of giants.' Your technology gave birth to everything they're doing now."

With a shaking hand, Woody took a sip of water. "That's the thing. Science by its very nature evolves through time. Who cares about the buggy whip of old? The cassette recorder? Push lawn mowers? Edison's record player that used wax cylinders? Last night I had a revelation, a disturbing one. Nothing lasts forever—nothing. A big explosion in Paris recently wiped out a bunch of historical buildings and according to yesterday's newspaper, the Hubble telescope is having heart attacks worse than mine. Nothing lasts forever, except..."

Angie leaned closer to Woody. "Except?"

"I have a hope that Socrates, Plato and Aristotle will go on, but I'm not sure. Nobody cares about those guys anymore. But I have favorites who might hang on." Woody coughed fitfully.

"Who? What?"

"I'm surprised you can't guess. Why is it I got sucked into the whirlpool of music? Me—a computer nut. Beethoven's Ninth is as close to eternal as can be. Perhaps Pachelbel's Canon in D and Mozart's Requiem. A Strauss waltz." Woody sucked in a deep breath. "Music has a power over me. They all stir my mind and make my heart pound. I get all sentimental. You brought all that to me, you know."

Angie choked back tears. "You are a true renaissance man, my love. Yes, I believe as long as there are violins to play, those pieces will be played. I also believe your website for BSO inspired listeners world-wide to embrace those composers and prolong their significance. Don't disregard the significance of your contributions."

Woody coughed again and clutched his chest.

"Are you okay?" Angie cried. "Should I call the nurse?"

Gasping for breath, Woody waved his hand. "No. It's going away already. Been doing this off and on all night. Ah, there. See? I'm fine."

"You scared me to death. I don't care what you say, I'm going to find the doctor and tell him what's happening. There was difficulty during your surgery, remember? Something about the stent not seating exactly right."

"The doctor didn't seem all that worried; he just wanted to keep me in the hospital a few extra days. It's no use to bother him, but if it makes you happy." He drew a big breath of relief. "Say, aren't Quad and Sheri coming to see me today?"

Angie rose from her chair and headed to the door. "Yes. I expect them in a little while, but I'll let them stay only if the doctor says it's okay."

A look of pleasure creased Woody's face. "Good. I've missed them. You run your silly errand and maybe I'll try to doze a little. Sleepless nights are terrible."

Angie learned that the doctor was in surgery, so she cornered the nurse. "My husband is having chest pains from time to time. Is that serious?"

The nurse put on her practiced facial expression—a mixture of disdain and impatience. "Mr. Lawrence had a heart attack and surgery. Pains are to be expected. He's on a morphine drip to control his discomfort, but we don't want to increase the dosage unless it's necessary because he'll become confused."

Morphine. Is that why he's having all those weird thoughts? Obviously not getting satisfactory information, Angie gave a tight-lipped smile and said, "Thanks." She returned to Woody's bedside, found him asleep, and began to read.

Outside, the storm continued to rage, flinging growling gusts of wind that rattled the window. Oddly, the tumult didn't waken Woody who whimpered softly behind closed eyes.

An hour later, Angie heard the easy chatter of Quad and Sheri coming down the hall.

As they walked in, they murmured greetings, "Hi, Mom."

Woody stirred. "They're here?"

"Yes, dear. Both are right here."

Quad stopped mid-room and stared at his father. Dressed in a tailored three-piece suit and polished imported shoes, he contrasted sharply to the withered, ashen figure in the bed. "Hi, Dad. You're looking good."

"You lie like all lawyers," Woody scowled.

"I brought you something," Quad said. "It's one of those smart speakers. I know you like Beethoven and such. If you want to listen to some fancy music, all you have to do is say, 'Alexa, play Beethoven.' And it does."

"Alexa? What's that?"

"It's the name of the speaker. She'll tell you the weather, football scores – anything."

"Hmmm. Might give it a try. Beethoven, Bach, Strauss..."

Quad set it on the bedside stand and plugged it in. "I'll lend you my phone until I can set up an account on yours."

At thirty-five, Sheri was two years younger than her husband. Dressed like a high school student, she looked fresh and vivacious. She stepped over to the bed and kissed her father-in-law on the cheek. "You old grump. For once, try being nice to Quad. So what if he's a lawyer; he makes a good living."

Woody chuckled. "They say every generation rebels against their parents, making them favor their grandparents. So Quad and Gramps became matches. I have to admit, with my son around it's like having the old man back. We had our differences, but I miss him."

A tinkling laugh brought a twinkle to Sheri's eyes. "I wish I'd gotten to know him. You've said he had a few tales to tell about Quad as a kid."

"That he did. Embarrassing it was," Quad said. "He was a crusty old fart but he loved the law. He inspired me."

Angie watched her family banter with joy. Her son had become a talented attorney in a large law firm and married a beautiful woman. Sadly, there had been no children, so the hope for Woodrow the Fifth had faded. Like Angie, Sheri went into the world of education and taught literature at a nearby high school. Judging from the laughter and repartee around the bed, the couple somehow arrived at a rewarding destination.

"Seriously, Dad, when are the doctors going to let you out of here?" Quad asked. "I worry about the complications with your surgery. What are they saying?"

Feebly, Woody waved his hand. "No big deal. I bet I'm discharged tomorrow."

"Not until your pains stop," Angie said. She turned to her son. "He's right. The doctor doesn't seem concerned, saying that stent procedures have become common."

"Pains you said? How bad?"

"Oh, they're nothing," Woody insisted. "What's to be expected when they shove a tube up your crotch into your heart?"

"What's all this?" growled the nurse, striding into the room. "You know that regulations limit ICU visitors to only one at a time."

Quad flashed an annoyed glance at the nurse. "What's the harm?"

"Rules are rules," retorted the woman. "Two of you will have to leave."

"Well, I have a big case to prepare. Sheri and I will take our leave." Quad strode over to Woody and patted his shoulder. "Be sure and try Alexa. You'll love her."

"We'll come see you again tomorrow, one at a time it sounds like," Sheri said.

They all said their good-byes.

Striding down the hall, Quad turned to Sheri and said, "Dad looks worn out. I hope the hospital can pump some magic into him."

* * *

After another sleepless night, Woody was pleased when Angie walked in. He laboriously sat up and kissed his wife. Easing back in the bed, he said, "Same thing last night—my life in review. Our son is my legacy and I hardly know him. It isn't that Quad became a lawyer; it's I never took him to ride go-karts. Never played catch with him." Woody rubbed his nose and frowned with a twinge of pain. "It seems like our careers got between us and the kid. We kept handing him off to babysitters."

"He turned out fine. We were good providers."

"Not enough…" Woody grabbed his chest and grunted. "Another pain! It's pretty bad!"

Angie snatched the call button and pressed it frantically. Woody began to writhe, so Angie bolted to the hall and cornered a nurse who, after quickly checking Woody, summoned a doctor.

With the predictable smile and cheerful voice, the doctor strode to Woody's bedside asking, "Well, well what seems to be the matter?"

"Another of my chest pains. Seemed a little worse than usual, but it's almost gone now."

"Mmmm." The doctor ceremoniously placed a stethoscope on Woody's chest and listened. Then he examined the monitors and nodded. "No real change. I can increase the morphine drip a bit if you'd like. What do you say?"

Woody thought a moment and said, "A bit? That isn't going to stop these pains—just turn my brain to mush. What else can you do?"

"Not much, I'm afraid. I'm having a specialist in Los Angeles studying those CT scans we took. I should know more in a day or two."

"They've had them since yesterday," Angie said. "Can you call this specialist and prod him?"

"She's a her, but I'll call. Meantime, no excitement. Just rest."

Angie fluffed Woody's pillow and straightened the blankets. "Why don't you get some sleep? I'll sit here and read, okay?"

Woody gazed at his wife and love flooded his thoughts. *I'm a lucky man.* He closed his eyes and fell asleep within moments.

While the storm had passed the day before, lingering clouds were black and menacing. Gloom covered the window, casting the room into darkness. Having gone without a meal all day, Angie's stomach growled. She looked at Woody once more and smiled. He rested easily even though his face looked drawn. She closed her book and stood, stiff from sitting so long. A soft pat on Woody's pillow signaled her farewell for the night. She crept quietly from the room, smiled at the night nurse and headed home.

Hours later, Woody's eyes sought the wall clock. *Ten after eleven. Now what?* The monitors beeped and flashed their green wiggly lines, annoying him. Another spasm struck and he reached for a glass of water. As before, the pain abruptly passed and then he noticed Quad's smart speaker on the bedside stand. *Plays music, he'd said. I'll try something – maybe a Strauss waltz. That would put me in a mellow mood, calm my nerves, and fill my head with joy.* "Alexa, play Strauss."

Within seconds, music filled the room. It wasn't a waltz, but a flute bubbled in accompaniment to violins. *Nice. The power of music will cure my ailments.* Woody leaned back and closed his eyes. Immersed in the notes, fresh thoughts danced in his head. *I suppose it's usual for guys pushing sixty to wonder what they've contributed to the ledger of life. Perhaps my greatest achievement was offering the Gateway kids a way to listen to orchestras.* He rubbed his chin, in deep in through. *Take that Jack Trumbo fellow. Who would have guessed that he'd sign up for Angie's music class and then go on to be the manager of the Melrose symphony. I can only repeat myself – I'll be damned.* Once more, Strauss' music captured Woody's conscience and he breathed in a sigh of intense pleasure.

Soon, the monitors stopped beeping and the wiggly lines wavered and became straight. The pinched look around Woody's mouth and the harsh creases around his eyes faded. Strauss' *Death and Transfiguration* swept over him and drifted through the doorway into the hall. Harsh alarms blared, bringing the doctor at a run.

The End

www.ingramcontent.com/pod-product-compliance
Lightning Source LLC
LaVergne TN
LVHW050527160826
845677LV00011B/1969